#11: Animals
January 2021

> Animals are such agreeable friends—they ask no questions; they pass no criticisms.
>
> *George Eliot*

CH - ANIMALS

Editorial

Editors-In-Chief: Mickey Collins & Robert Eversmann

Managing Editors: Ariel Kusby, Michael Santiago & Z.B. Wagman

Poetry: Ariel Kusby & Jihye Shin

Prose: Azalea Micketti, Michael Santiago & Z.B. Wagman

Cover: Kezia Rasmussen & Zuriel van Belle

Contact: editors@deepoverstock.com
deepoverstock.com

ON THE SHELVES

7 The Temp - Walter Moon

9 Traumatic Indoctrination - Robert Torres

18 Just Another Crow - Yuan Changming

19 Keeper of the Realm - Fabrice Poussin

20 The Deer - Bob Selcrosse

22 Kitty - Jonathan van Belle

23 Leaving the Slaughterhouse - Lynette G. Esposito

24 Golden Eyes - Michael Baldwin

25 The We Hate Animals Club - Arnold B. Cabdriver

29 Forest of Arden - Desiree Ducharme

36 Cousin in Florida - John Grey

37 Marport - Zuriel van Belle

40 We May Never Remove Our Masks around the Monkeys - Arnold B. Cabdriver

41 Hospital for Reanimated Pets - Kellye McBride

46 The Duck - Eric Thralby

48 A Small Group of Fishermen - Arnold B. Cabdriver

51 Meow - Jonathan van Belle

53 You Don't Say - Fabrice Poussin

54 Rescue - Desiree Ducharme

57 Dytiscus Larvae: a Dramatic Scene - Yuan Changming

58 Black Bird - Ariel Kusby

59 The Cormorant - Sarah Bartlett

62 Frog Calls - Yuan Changming

63 Fireflies - Z.B. Wagman

65 The Bone - Michal Goldstein

66 Menagerie, shop window, Paris - Roger Camp

67 Blackberry Epiphany - Michael Baldwin

68 Elegy to the Great Auk - Yuan Changming

69 Hummingbird - G Michael Smith

70 Nice Place - Fabrice Poussin

71 Gongxifacai [恭喜发财]: An Idiomatic Chinese Calendar - Yuan Changming

72 Or Was it Not a Koi - Sarah Bartlett

73 Cat for Cole - Mickey Collins

75 Saved by Cats - AJD

continued...

76 The Golden Brown Dog - Nicholas Yandell

78 Black Birds in the Backyard - Lynette G. Esposito

79 My Cat - George White

81 Pig & Cat - Roger Camp

82 Story of Sabi - Heather Glover

89 Gharial: A Riddle Poem - Marlowe Whittenberg

91 Day 5 - Chipmunks - Esther Fishman

93 Early Evening - Lynette G. Esposito

94 Horse Sculpture - Roger Camp

Letter from the Editors

Dearest Readers,

Meow, woof, squeak! That's just the animal way of saying wow we got a lot of great submissions. We could fill a zoo, but we wouldn't because these stories shouldn't be caged; they're free-range!

Inside this issue you'll find cats, deer, ducks, monkeys, chipmunks, fireflies, a whole assortment of birds, fish, dogs, and more! No(ah) one got more animals than us. Enjoy reading them to your own furry friends (animal or human).

Issue 12 is sure to bring surprises and maybe make you go, "Huh?" We're moving from the extinct to the instinct, from what crawls under foot to what is afoot, from the family pet on a leash to crime-solving cats finding leads. It's Mysteries!

Submit your mystery piece or pieces by February 28th (or will it be?). We look forward to solving them (or will we?).

Best,

Deep Overstock Editors

The Temp
by Walter Moon

The Temp, something I did not ask for, is here. Like most humans, It's tall and lumbering, and oh Bast, It's speaking in kitten-talk already. One of my roommates, a young kitten my human roommates call "Lucy" (whom I have yet to give my blessing to), is already performing for the new creature, cautiously trying to introduce herself. So desperate.

Do my human roommates think we're unable to take care of ourselves? I can easily get to my food and it wouldn't be the first time I used my claws to open a can. While Lucy has gone on to begin her usual morning routine of scratching everything and running around, behaviors I have never understood, the lumbering giant has gone over to wake up Missy (she sleeps through everything). The Temp looks horrified that Missy isn't moving or responding to Its "speaking" but I rather enjoy Its confused terror.

Of course, Missy is fine, and as soon as she is awake she is also acting excited that there is a stranger in our home. The awkward Temp opens the door to let Missy, who has proven herself unable to use a litter box, outside to do her business. I go and wait by the door, ready to explain that we are fine on our own and would prefer that our human roommates return, if there must be a human here at all.

Lucy has crouched by the door behind the curtain waiting to attack the giant upon reentry; little does she know It is now chasing Missy around the yard trying to help detach the unmentionable from her backside that seems to be hanging there somehow, as Missy herself tries to avoid stepping on a snail. The dignity of human and canine on full display. Bast help me.

As It reenters the house with Missy, both looking unreasonably pleased to have solved their little quandary, I begin to make my request, but of course not before It calls me "Fluff Boy." Excuse me? My human roommates call me "Niko," thank you. My real name? You could never possibly pronounce it in your so-called human "words."

Missy has begun to explain to the Temp that she in fact can have as many treats as she wants, contrary to the note left for It that It has now read aloud to her. It puts our food out and refreshes our water, after which I would assume It would leave. But no! Of course not, that would be too simple. Too much to ask.

An hour later, It is still here. Eating popcorn that It did not bring, and watching the cartoon Thundercats on the couch. Is this to mock me? Cats that look and talk in human-speak? Please. Lucy and Missy have become full blown traitors, sitting on either side of It, doing what I have heard my human roommates call "cuddling." Disgusting.

Finally, It gets up after being here for three hours (a completely unnecessary amount of time) and babbles something about being here tomorrow. Bast take me, now. After calling me "Fluffle Daddy," Missy "Magoo" (wow rude), and Lucy "Rascal" (is this creature purposely trying to piss me off?), It exits through the garage, hopefully not planning to make good on Its threat to return again.

Traumatic Indoctrination
by Robert Torres

Billy was a good Christian as he walked to school. Billy had been a good Christian all weekend and for the last four years since his mom let him get baptized at the tender age of 7. He was glad to have direction in his life and he carried God's love with him like an omnipresent security blanket. It made him a bit of a prick but Billy had enough friends for a sixth grader. His favorite subject was science. He didn't dwell much on the contradictions between his pastor's lectures and Mrs. Simmons' geology lessons. He liked to picture dinosaurs roaming the earth and leaving huge paw prints behind; he didn't care how long ago it happened.

Today, Mrs. Simmons wasn't in. There was a substitute with square black glasses and a ponytail.

"Hello, my name is Mr. Fowler." Billy didn't like substitutes. Billy didn't like watching videos or Bill Nye the Science Guy or change. "Mrs. Simmons will be out for a while. She's on something called 'administrative leave.' She was trying to unionize. Not but be confused with un-ionize!" Mr. Fowler laughed. The children were dumbfounded.

"Now, I know when you all saw me, you were looking forward to a day of watching videos, but we're going to be together for a while, so I want to jump right back into what you've been studying!" *A ray of hope*, Billy thought, *a substitute who isn't a layabout!* "According to Mrs. Simmons' syllabus, you've been studying taxonomy, the different kinds of plants and animals."

"And bugs!" cried Sam, the redhead who Billy hated in a stare-at-him-all-class sort of way.

Mr. Fowler asked for Sam's name, then asked the difference between animals and bugs.

"Bugs have exoskeletons!"

"That's very true." Mr. Fowler said. "They have exoskeletons, but they're still animals. They're a kind of invertebrate." He wrote 'invertebrate' on the board. "What are some other kinds of animals?" Hands shot up.

"Birds!"

"Insects!"

"Mammals!"

"Snakes!"

Reptiles, Billy thought. He'd read the entire *D.K. Animal Encyclopedia* so he felt like his input would be cheating.

"Great! Let's look at some of the categories we already have: Birds, insects, mammals, and snakes. What sets them apart from each other?" No hands shot up this time, so after a few moments, Billy raised his.

"Mammals and birds are warm-blooded. Snakes are reptiles, so they're cold-blooded. Insects don't really have blood."

"That's a good start. What else?" Billy didn't realize the question was for the whole class, not just him, so he kept talking.

"Mammals give live birth. Birds and reptiles lay eggs that are already fertized—"

"Fertilized! Good." Billy would never forgive him now.

"Insects I guess spray their eggs and stuff all around like fish."

"Insects are very diverse and reproduce in a number of strange ways. Do you know what my favorite insects to study are, kids?" *How could we possibly know that, you fool*, thought Billy. "My favorites are bedbugs." The kids all said 'eww' with exaggeration. "Yes, they're nasty and they've become hard to kill because we've been trying to kill them for so long. But the way they breed is the most interesting thing about them. Male bedbugs use a specialized sex organ to mate and sometime females don't get to use theirs at all. Instead, the males clobber their way in any old place in the female's exoskeleton, and shoot their *gametes* into their *hemolymph*." These last two science words, he over-annunciated but didn't bother putting on the board. The class sat in stunned silence. Billy gingerly raised his hand.

"Does it...does it hurt them?"

"Oh yes! They run from it. Some of them die from infections in the wounds, especially if they've had multiple partners."

"Why don't they do it like normal bugs?"

"We don't know. They have sex organs like other animals, but somewhere down the line it became easier for them to survive if they did it this way. It's how they *evolved*."

Yes, Billy thought, *this is evolution's fault*, not God's. Mr. Fowler moved on to talking about bees and ants. Billy clammed up for the rest of class. He clammed up during lunch, during math and Spanish classes, too. He only opened his mouth for chorus class because he knew his fellow tenors were counting on him. Billy's peers in chorus, however, would probably have agreed on one thing: Billy's voice was like an unpopped popcorn kernel: utterly impossible to ignore and absolutely unwanted.

The final bell rang. Billy, unlike most middle schoolers, lived close enough to school to walk. Normally, he lamented missing out on the chance to socialize on the bus, but on days like today when his mind has something to chew on, it was good to be walking alone.

He came home. He microwaved a snack and ate it. He spread his homework out in front of him. His father came home, said hello, and ordered dinner. His mother came home. They ate together. His parents asked about school. Billy told them about the new song they learned in chorus. They watched TV together for an hour or so after dinner. They all went to bed.

This is when Billy was seized by the fear. God had built a

creature that stabs its partner to make more. Or, he let evolution run so far off course that they popped out on their own. Billy wasn't sure which was worse. Billy wondered what God had in store for humans. He also wondered if he had bedbugs. He had never even seen one. He sat up and turned to look at his sheets. It was too dark to see anything. He couldn't turn on the light or his father would yell. He remembered the streetlight. It shined so brightly into his room that his father had put up a blackout curtain. Billy pulled back that curtain but now that he needed it, the light seemed dimmer than before. Still, it was bright enough to make out the creases and folds of his sheets. He didn't see anything moving around, so he tousled his sheets as quietly as he could to see if he could scare something into moving. He didn't see anything. *Are they microscopic? Could they be on me already?* Billy thought not, since he didn't have any irregular itching. He left the curtain open and got back into bed. He kept peeking down at the sheets until he drifted off to sleep.

    The sound of a great windstorm rattling the siding of the house roused Billy from some deep dream. The whole house creaked but the power lines and trees outside were still. Then, a dark but shiny mass appeared in the window. A huge insectoid leg tapped on the window, then struck it hard enough to shatter the glass. Billy shivered as the shards sprayed across his room. The creature blocked out the light as it squeezed its body through the window. Its inflexible carapace tore away first the glass remaining in the frame and then the frame itself and the wall surrounding as it pulled itself in. It took a painfully long time, but Billy was paralyzed with fear, not even able to call out to his parents or God. Certainly not God, who Billy was certain had sent this beast against him for questioning the divine plan. Just as Billy had let the devil into his thoughts, so the creator had let this monster into his room.

    The light from outside returned at the insect's body plunked to the floor. Its antennae swayed back and forth like divining rods. Billy hoped that since he couldn't move the bug might just ignore him, but it moved right away towards the bed. Its foreleg cracked the footboard as it got on the bed. Billy now saw what swung between its hind legs: a coarse, spike-covered club, a genital perfectly evolved for bashing in an exoskeleton and probably pretty darn effective at bashing in something soft like, for instance, human flesh. The insect leaned forward and the club swung down on the bed, tearing up the bedsheets. *Please, don't let it realize it missed*, thought Billy, still unable to speak or move. The insect seemed to sense his fear and pulled out. It took a few steps forward, then struck again, this time hitting Billy square in the belly. The pain was crushing. Billy couldn't scream if he wanted to now because his lungs couldn't inflate, his diaphragm was now punctured by the monster and slowly being pumped with some kind of fluid. *It wants to fertilize my hemolymph*, thought Billy, *but I haven't got any*. As the pressure increased, so did the searing pain in Billy's body cavity. Soon he had no room for any thoughts at all. The animal retracted itself and blood started pumping out of the wound. The monster began to shrink, first from the size of the bed to the size of a pillow, then to the size of Billy's palm, then the size of a grain of rice, and then it fell and burrowed into the bedsheets. Billy lay with the hot burning all inside of him. Still unable to breathe, he was crying silently. *God must be very mad at me*, Billy thought, just before passing out.

When he woke up, the first thing he noticed was not the absence of pain, but the absence of wind. The window was still intact. He sat up in bed. The wound was gone. He thought it was all a terrible dream, but as he looked to inspect his footboard he instead saw that a large plant had sprung up from between his legs. He was attached to it by a small root that led up somewhere inside of his bum. A bright yellow light illuminated the stalk from the hole the plant had punched in the ceiling. Billy was afraid of the root that attached him to the plant, but as he moved, he couldn't feel it at all. He took a deep breath and pulled it free from the plant. As soon as he did, it withered away as if set on fire.

Well, I suppose I ought to climb, thought Billy, *and ask whoever planted this thing to get rid of it and fix the hole in the ceiling*. The plant was studded all over with young branches, which made it easy climbing for Billy. As soon as his feet were off his bed, the plant began to grow again. It shot him up out of his bedroom before he could jump off. He passed the broken drywall of his ceiling, then the insulation in the attic and the shingles of the roof. His house shrank away from him as his neighborhood came into view. It was nearly dawn and the eastern sky was bright with the sun hiding just around the corner. The light above Billy was even brighter, though, and Billy still couldn't see the source. The plant grew so high that Billy crashed into the cloud line and then he couldn't see much. He had the distinct feeling of being underwater and on instinct held his breath. After a few seconds, he felt himself surfacing. He took a breath, opened his eyes, and saw before him a vast cloudscape. Suddenly the plant became too weak to hold him and wilted over, depositing him on the surface of clouds. Billy wasn't too surprised that they had a surface. He'd spent a lot of time picturing heaven with the help of the paintings at church. The light that had illuminated the plant down on earth was hidden behind a castle-like pillar of cloud in front of him.

Rounding the corner, Billy struggled to take in what he saw: gold rings of light swirling with each other, spinning and orbiting some imperceptible point in their middle. Each ring was studded all over with pairs of eyes with black square-rimmed glasses. Their spinning was chaotic. The light was brighter than the sun but it didn't hurt Billy's eyes, which was good because the light was inescapable and cast no shadows.

"Step forward, child." Despite its volume, the voice was warm and inviting.

"G-G-God?" Billy stuttered in awe.

"Shame on you, that your faith is so weak you would mistake the Lord itself for a mere agent."

"I'm sorry. Do you have a name?"

"Pravuil"

"But what's your real name?" A gust of hot wind emanated from the center of the angel. It made Billy's skin feel hot and dry.

"Oh, like, I can't pronounce it, because I'm human?"

"No. That was your warning for asking rude questions. My only name is Pravuil."

"I'm sorry." Billy imagined this was what being pulled into the principal's office felt like.

"You were brought here that you might better understand the nature of God."

"But the nature of God is love."

"God has no use for love."

"That's an awful thing to say. Everybody needs love. That's why we have God." Billy was starting not to trust this angel. Billy worried, *is distrusting an angel the same as distrusting God?*

"God does not answer to your needs. God creates your ability to need."

"Did god create bed bugs the way they are, too?"

"God is the vacuum they filled by evolving." Billy turned this over in his mind.

"So God carved a space for them to fill and let them grow into it?"

"God is the absence that allows for your presence."

"God is....absence?" That didn't sit right with Billy. By his pastor's reckoning, God was presence, not absence, since he was everywhere. God is omni-*present*, not omni-*absent*.

"God is the infinite void into which your chaos spills."

"Chaos? We've got all kinds of order! Like DNA! It's re-writing itself all the time."

"And yet it gave you bedbugs." Billy was stumped, and a little disgusted to have to keep talking about them.

"Well, they're only like that because they're coded that

Traumatic Indoctrination 15

way."

"The bedbugs are self-replicating chaos." Billy was beginning to feel for the little bugs. It wasn't their fault they mate the way they mate. It wasn't fair for this awful, immaterial entity to say mean things about all of those burdened with bodies.

"Well so I am! I'm chaos too!" Billy charged for the center of the angel. Pravuil's rings all aligned to form a large disc and from the center came an expansive void that enveloped Billy. From the intense light, he was plunged directly into an endless darkness. Billy felt himself still moving in the direction he had been running, but there were no stars or other lights to refer to. It was awfully cold, so cold that Billy had a hard time remembering what it was ever like to be warm. *Am I dying?* Billy thought. *The bedbug killed me and I failed the angel's test so it threw me out into this void to float forever.* Billy wished he could apologize to God. Billy had expected fire and shackles and cackling demons with spears and whips. That all seemed exciting. Awful and painful yes but still, it was something to see. In this hell, Billy was alone with his thoughts and the darkness and the cold.

Just as Billy's spirit was hitting rock bottom, a point of light shone in the darkness. For a long time, it was no bigger than a star in the night sky, but after a little while longer of floating, Billy came upon it. It was only a few millimeters long, but the light shining from it was so bright and so perfect that Billy could make out every detail of its carapace, the margins of its exoskeleton, the sections of its antennae, right down to the spines along its tiny legs. It was a bedbug, and it was perfect. *This is much nicer than the angel*, Billy thought. *Why didn't this thing come say hi to me instead?* Staring into the bedbug's light, Billy could see everything. He saw his own birth and a small rodent giving birth to its small litter. He saw man's first step on the moon and some alien species stepping off an alien rocket onto an alien moon. He saw a first kiss, an envelope drop into a mailbox, a tree explode with lightning deep in a forest, a thousand families sitting down to television, a million farmers pulling roots from the earth, and the endless mechanizations of the heavens churning throughout time. Billy understood now. The void was what let the light in. Everything that tended to make more of itself ended up doing so until another part of the chaos swallowed it up. The void got bigger and bigger as the chaos did. The void would always be enough for us. This was the infinity of God's power in action. Billy cried tears of joy. He wanted to reach out and embrace the luminescent bug, but as he tried, he realized he was already in contact with it. He began to descend, carrying its light with him.

He fell for a while through blackness lit only by the insect, then nothing at all, then, slowly, stars populated the void. Eventually the earth, opulent in green and blue, appeared below. Under the swirls of clouds, he could make out North America as he hurtled towards it. *This must be my town coming towards me*, thought Billy. Just as he was able to make out his house, he crashed through his roof and into his bed. The heat and light of God still radiated off of him.

When he woke, he felt perfectly well rested. The holes in his roof and wall were repaired, as was his bed frame and sheets. His mother was knocking on the door, saying he was late for school. He blushed as he noticed a mess in his pants.

Just Another Crow
by Yuan Changming

Still, still hidden
Behind old shirts and pants
Like an inflated sock
Hung on a slanting coat hanger

With a prophecy stuck in its throat
Probably too dark or ominous
To yaw, even to breathe

No one knows when or how
It will fly out of the closet, and call

Keeper of the Realm - Fabrice Poussin

The Deer
by Bob Selcrosse

The Deer I

They would fire on three.
Red leaves, yellow leaves, green leaves.
The shot—like the birth of his son.
The leaves.
The animal.

The son cowered in the bushes.
The father took the son's gun and counted.
One through six bullets.
The son had not fired the gun.
Leaves clicked as the deer bled through them.
Now—the father was a fool.

The Deer II

The beauty of a deer split cleanly.
The split smells a tree, as if you've cut a log.
The parts of the deer are separated from the deer.
The pieces, detached from the deer, do not bleed on their own.
They are arranged logically on a tarp.
The deer must be cleaned. And then the gun must then be cleaned.
The gun is disassembled on a table above the deer.
It is all put back into pieces.
This is gorgeous in the case of the gun and the deer.
The father was not a caveman.
He made precise heavy cuts.
The son put his hands in the deer.
The son's hand filled with pearls.

The Deer III

A father and son see a deer full of tumors and call animal control.
Animal control says that, if, and only if, a tumor falls on the ground, will they come.
Finally, a tumor is found in the leaves and there is a trail of blood.

The father and son follow the blood into the woods.
This is in the middle of Fall. It smells like leaves. The leaves are everywhere. There are leaves on the ground. There are leaves in the trees.
The deer is in a clearing, alone, eating leaves.
The father and son see it.
The son falls over. The shock of the deer.
The father goes to the deer.
The deer falls over. The shock of cancer.
Everywhere, the deer is swollen.
The father takes the deer by the antlers.
He must do it. If he does not do it, the deer will take days to die.
The father is watched by the son.
The father, using the grip of the antlers, turns.
It is not unlike turning a ship.

Kitty
by Jonathan van Belle

Her white treble hooks hook hearts;
a cat must dice, ever since the vegan lion was disparadised

Lil' Red-in-Tooth, dear kitty preening,
comes clawed and fond of cleaving

Fond of me
in a dish

With eyes moon-round, the Egyptian queen,
like Mephistopheles, springs out

O, but oh look, oh,
our dozing darling fiend,
how she purrs,
how she's a purring donut

Does Precious dream?

Yes, of gutting,
of flensing and filleting;
of everything, bloodied, fleeing, screaming

Into every open wound
her heart-shaped nose dips, then drips;
Soft dreaming, kitty sneezes blood, and roars a purr

Only for eating, then excreting,
does she deign adjourn the sweet hell in her

Leaving the Slaughterhouse
by Lynette G. Esposito

I was riding a blind horse down the center of town
Horns honked
Women screamed
Men heehawed mouths wide
open--
all I could see is calamity;
the horse saw nothing,
followed the guidance of my gentle
nudge of the reins on his neck
showing him his way home
after cashing in the winning
Lottery ticket.

Golden Eyes
by Michael Baldwin

Toads are unlovely: plump, bumpy, gawkward.
But I've been fond of them since I was young.
Their inoffensive, comical dignity amused me.
Gaze into a toad's lovely golden eyes
and you quickly become its friend.

Why, then, did I shoot a toad in my backyard when,
age twelve, I had invented a slingshot that propelled
the sharp-ended rib of a broken umbrella like an arrow?
What ancient hunter-killers abide within our genes,
eager to emerge, to erase our innocence?

Poor, dumb creature, belly-skewered by the tine,
but, no blood, no writhing, no squeal of pain.
Its golden eyes gazed into mine and slowly blinked,
as if unbelieving. I eased the rod from its body,
placed the stoic toad near a fence corner, and slunk away.

Next day, its golden eyes were gone to empty sockets,
stiff corpse grotesque with dying agonies,
stolid toadish dignity ravaged by red ants.
I broke the slingshot and buried it with my friend.

Nowadays, there are fewer toads than in my youth,
decimated by pesticides, environmental degradation,
casual cruelty. I did not tell my mother of the killing.
She might have said its golden eyes were God's.

The We Hate Animals Club
by Arnold B. Cabdriver

Sundays we take Mikey to the zoo to fuck with the monkeys. We dress him like a monkey and lean him on the glass.

You'll never be as smart as me, says Mikey. No matter what you think, you'll never think like I think, he says.

The baboon sits on a high branch.

Cocksucker, says Mikey.

The baboon does not look at Mikey, but into its own puffy hands.

Mikey turns back to us. I bet his face got jacked up and he's afraid to show it, he says. He bangs on the glass and calls the monkey a shit-eater and a coward.

Mikey stands on the handrail and leans his face on the glass. You've got nothing to look forward to, he says. Look at me. He bangs on the glass.

A fat man speaks to us like we're his children. You are monsters, he says.

Mikey is about to rip the man's cock off. We take him to the hippos. Mikey doesn't give a shit about the hippos.

For me, I do not mind the monkeys. They lick their own fingers which are covered in shit.

What's more: there is no reason for the prairie dog.

It digs in dirt and infests holes with babies.

I will show you. Here, I have with me a taped sandwich bag which I have filled with cayenne pepper.

Watch me as I take it and stand on Mikey's back and dirty the monkey with my feet.

The prairie dog enclosure is plexiglass. It is about six-by-six feet full of dirt. There is a tiny family, standing very straight and leaning a little to the side.

I untape the bag and dump the red contents inside. I cayenne the prairie dogs.

At first they are curious. They come with their paws and their mouths and their eyes.

But when it touches their skin, immediately they curl like bugs and try to scratch off their faces. They dig through the dirt until they're stopped by the glass.

C'est la vie. Que sera sera.

Three idiot boy scouts in blue shorts and yellow scarves are holding a spider next to a zookeeper in an expired green shirt and a big khaki hat. Three boys touching their fingertips and throning a spider. They all look into it and say wow. It's just there so they can touch each other. They are a bunch of hiccuping butt-ticklers.

The zookeeper starts some bullshit about spiders.

One of the boy scouts, with a bracelet and a scowl like a deformity, says, like it's a challenge, We're the Boy Scouts of America.

The one to his left says, Pack two-two-two. He is a kid in a baseball cap and zoo animal backpack that was a leash at one point.

Pack two-two-two, says Eric. He pinches the kid.

The zookeeper knows we're something to avoid but asks us, would we like to touch the spider?

You hand-fuck that spider all you want, I say.

The boy scouts look at their hands and stare into the spider. It is as if, for the first time, they are afraid of their own hands.

They are the kind of dead scum that grow up and have kids of their own. They are the kind of shit of the earth that look up to their fathers, do their fathers proud, read books and grow up to be their fathers. We look long and hard into our futures. We are only concerned with how shitty the animal kingdom is.

Eric hates anything larger than a human being. We call him "the whale."

We will bring him to what he hates. But there are many things in the zoo.

"The whale" wants to move on.

Eric hates elephants. His hate is strong and old like elephants. You can see it in his body, getting close to them, his body gets like it's suddenly infected.

When we get to the elephants he freezes. His hate becomes still and pure as desert wind. He cannot move if he's got his eyes on an elephant.

We buy two strawberry milkshakes and climb onto the observation deck. The enclosure is very high and very large. The elephants sweep bits of the ground into their mouths, but otherwise stand still as tables. We milkshake the elephants. We have destroyed the elephants in the eyes of the people. Now they are nothing, they are pink and filthy.

A kid with a lion backpack that still is a leash, pushes his painted face up against the glass, his mom holding the leash. We're going to throw him in the lion pit.

The We Hate Animals Club

Wow, I say. So cool. Mikey says, Lions are the best. Eric leans into the safety railing and jumps up and down. Roar already! he says. The kid's mom smiles at us, she's on the phone. Three little boys, she says. They like the lions too. Everybody likes the lions.

Mikey gives me his knife. I get behind the kid and cut the leash off his backpack.

We go to see the dumbest animal of any zoo, the sun bear. I hate the sun bear most of all.

The sun bear thinks it's everyone's little brother.

The idiot lumbers over. I beat the glass and remind it it's too dumb to kill itself. It yawns and sits beside the glass.

I hate the animal population because it continues, it survives, and it does not know how stupid it looks.

The sun bear, king of assholes, presses its paw on the glass against my hand. Its eyes widen, then it rolls out its ten-inch tongue.

Forest of Arden
by Desiree Ducharme

The trees are old in the forest of Arden. They hold many secrets. The greenest grow at the border of the tame world. Supple firs and bendy pines peak above sprawling hardwoods. Tall, wide oaks dot the perimeter charming the senses with song birds and the fluffy-tailed squirrels. Lush moss carpets the fallen. Ferns share the barracks of mycological troops. Raptors rest in the crowns of conifers. From this vantage point, their keen eyes watch the aspens sough in the meadows that surround the heart. The soft rustling of green an auditory sign post for bat and owl. The harsher clacking of gold in autumn a gentle warning to those who journey past them.

The animals kept the trees' secrets and the trees kept theirs. An owl watched the shadow of a bear in the moonlight. The bear smelled of bear. It was a familiar smell. Part predator, part protection. Fear and blood mixed with death and safety. Its full winter coat made it appear even more massive than it was. Or maybe that was a trick of age. It moved quickly but unhurried through the trees. Despite its size, it made noise only when it wanted. The leaves did not crackle or crunch beneath the huge paws. It was a shadow moving through shadows. There was a small child upon its back. It swayed gently with the roll and pitch of the bears' progress. The child, like the bear, smelled of death and safety. It exhaled winter from its lungs into the warm night. Fluffy ice pretending to be smoke. They were out of place in a place out of time.

Many forests become dense and impenetrable as you approach their wild hearts. Not Arden. Arden is barren at its core. Even the trees avoid the heart of Arden. An old burn, hot and furious, purged the balance long ago. Ancient flames sterilized the soil. The final circle of trees bare the wounds of light and heat. Wounds that never healed. Halfdead sentinels at the gateway to a graveyard. Hollowed out husks-turned-homes for the adaptable survivor. Lizards scurry over ash, caked and cracked on skeletal tree remains. Lichen clings to the boulders but has made little progress at restoration. A millennia of rains could not wash the rage from this place. Arden was a master's circle of arboreal survival spiraling outward to safety. At the center, a single rowan corpse stretches empty branches towards the sky.

Arkto could feel the child's hands in his fur. The same strange pressure he woke with in a different place, in a different time, when he was a different bear. Arkto recalled how he tried to get rid of it. He took it straight to the river. He remembered how it was finally dislodged when he shook on the far bank. It was a tiny thing. Much smaller than a bear cub. It lay shaking in the litter. Arkto could not smell it, which is troubling for a bear. A bear who can't smell has very few seasons left. Arkto cleared his snout several times then roared hoping to elicit the proper smells. The child planted its four scrawny limbs, cleared its snout a few times and screeched back at him. Annoyed and somewhat worried at the absence of fear scent, Arkto reared to his full height and startled most of the mountain with a second roar. The air filled with the fright of his woodland neighbors. He could even smell the wolverine on the far side, deep in its den. The child stood and screeched back at him. Arkto dropped down and stuck his nose directly into the child's soft center and inhaled. It smelled of rage and annoyance. It smelled like Arkto. Then it rumbled and patted Arkto. When Arkto returned to his den at sundown, the child was there.

The bear thought about that spring as they moved through the forest of Arden. Arkto the mighty, and his mostly-hairless cub. The child had been injured by its elders. They were terrified of bears so it felt the safest place to recover was with the biggest bear it could find. It taught Arkto how to disable and avoid the hunters' traps. It brought honey from the beehive he could not reach. They played pranks on the wolverine and the fox. It scratched the winter coat from Arkto. He enjoyed it. The child would climb onto Arkto and Arkto would climb the mountain. At the top, they would watch the stars. On the way down, the child would try to stand on his back while he ran. They howled with the wolves and rumbled. The moon after equinox brought news. The dangerous elders had left. The child could return to its own. Arkto remembered his den feeling hollow after. The child had grown though the bear could hardly feel its weight as he walked.

"Arkto, this is not our forest."

"I am aware you think that." The bear knew. The child had to find it within itself. "You left honey for me."

"I did."

"How many winters has it been?" The first time Arkto walked this forest was the winter the child came to him.

"Five in our forest. I don't think it is winter here. It smells like rain after a fire." He felt a shift. The child was standing. Its balance had improved. Its limbs were strong. Arkto rumbled and took a few paces at a gallop. The child rumbled joyfully, faltered but remained standing. Arkto slowed, his limbs were not as strong. "You are tired." The child smelled of concern.

"I have seen 36 winters. For a bear, that is a lot." Arkto was resigned.

"This one is my tenth. It feels like a lot." It was lowering its center. Arkto could feel it adjusting its weight through his shoulders.

"Humans." The bear chortled.

"Yes, but you nap through the terrible bits." It was laying on him now, scratching his ears. He loved when it scratched his ears.

"We all make choices. Bears are just smarter than humans." Arkto was grateful for the gentle strength of the child's fingers.

"I'm grateful for it. Is that why you didn't eat me?"

"Yes. You were scrawny. I thought your bones would be too spiky and get stuck in my teeth, like porcupine quills. I was hoping you'd fatten up over the summer. Why do you think I kept trying to get you to eat the salmon?"

"Was that why you kept slapping me with a fish and knocking me down river? Humans really are stupid."

"You were a slow learner."

"I am aware. Speaking of porcupines, how's the tail?"

"We promised never to talk about that."

"My bad. I'm just a stupid human." The child patted his head.

"You were smart enough to survive a winter as a bear."

"Well, I had a good teacher. If I was smarter, I would have stayed." Arkto felt the edges of regret scratching his cub's heart.

"You had to go. All cubs must make their own way." Truth did not sooth them. Change is the way of things. They were both aware that they were on different paths.

They moved in silence until they came to a meadow filled with aspens. The bear sat and the child slid from it. The bear and his child watched the stars for several minutes.

"How did we come to this place?"

"I cannot answer that."

"Bears." The child rolled its eyes. Arkto rumbled again.

"The first time I saw your eyes do that, I thought you had died."

"Really?"

"Yes. The eye rolling is a human expression. Bears do not have an equivalent." The child rumbled again.

"I always felt getting slapped in the face with a fish was the bear equivalent of the eye roll." They rumbled together for a time. "Arkto, I am scared. I feel I am at the edge of something that I cannot possibly endure." It nuzzled into his shoulder.

Arkto rolled back on his haunches and embraced it. The child still fit into his arms.

"I do not have a fish, child, but I feel you need me to slap you with one." He felt the tension release as it chortled.

"I'm serious you dumb bear. Not everything can be solved by knocking me down river." It was curling its toes around his claws. Arkto curled them upwards and the child curled its feet down. This small flexing and release had been a wonder to Arkto. Bears spend less than two winters as cubs. Male bears do not rear young. It makes them forget the simple discovery of how we fit into a space with others, how others fit into a space with us. The child's toes pulled slightly at the fur between his pads. Its feet were twice as big as they had been, yet still so tiny compared to the bear's. They were still curiously cold yet radiating heat into Arkto. Skin to skin, the only part of him not covered in fur. It was a unique sensation between him and the child. There was no other experience like it.

"Sometimes it helps. You always found your way back to the den. Which was annoying. Though that is the nature of cubs and so I was proud." The child was startled and looked at him with wide eyes. "What?"

"You were proud? Of me?"

"Of course I was. Stupid human. You found your own way. Every time you made it back to the den, I heard the bear within you." This was the truth of the child. A bear is a bear, you are what you are. Yet Arkto the Mighty found a bear inside a small child. The discovery was a wonder to them both.

"That was my stomach, growling in hunger. You dumb fur ball." Arkto slowly rose so the child was standing on its own. He nuzzled its soft center. It rumbled as it did the day they met.

"I felt your strength but smelled no fear. A cub becoming. I had never felt pride in something else's survival before, only my own. Pride in myself for surviving. You changed an old bear into something new. You found a way for us both." The child's face was leaking. Crying. The wind tried to snatch the tears but they clung to Arkto. As the strange child had. The wind could not separate bear from child either.

"I brought us here." It whispered. The bear nodded. "This is our forest while you are sleeping." He nodded again. "You are sleeping now, in your den." Dreaming. Arkto lay down and rolled to scratch his back. The ground was rocky here. The child watched him in the starlight. The wind lifted its hair. It closed its eyes and inhaled. The aspens softly applauded. An owl asked the question neither bear nor child could articulate. It echoed around them. The answer was close. The wind brought ash with it from the center.

"Child," The bear got to its feet. "My time in the world is ending."

"I know." The child climbed onto his back. "You are a part of this forest, if you wish." The owl questioned them again.

"I would like that very much." They began walking again in the direction of the answer. "Don't be lazy up there, scratch my ears." They rumbled together as the child scratched the bear's ears. Arkto knew the child would find a way to make this old forest new again. He could feel the fire within, smoldering just below the surface. He felt it in his paws when they touched the earth. Arkto followed it.

Arkto's paws sent swirls of ash into the air. He stopped. "I can go no further." The ash settled onto the fur at his feet.

"What happens now?"

"I cannot answer that."

"Ugh, bears." The child rolled its eyes.

"If I had a fish…" Arkto sat. The child clung to him.

"I will find my way back to the den." It whispered into the back of Arkto's neck. He could feel the tears. Arkto barked suddenly. It was strangely involuntary. He felt the absence of the child and smelled smoke on the wind. "Thank you, Arkto." The child kissed the bear between the eyes. They breathed each other. They walked the dream of their meeting. Arkto calling the earth through him like thunder, the child screeching. Arkto cleared his snout causing the child to smile, mostly smile. Together, they walked the trails in a distant wood, in a different season.

Smoke rose from the center of the rowan. They smelled it. The forest where they began arrived in the forest where they were. Resolve caught them. The child turned to face the tree. Resolve was sticky. It is one thing to decide to do a thing, it is quite another to begin. "Bring honey." He nudged it gently from behind. "Be what you are." The bear turned and walked back into the woods. The child looked back over its shoulder. The bear was gone. An owl called from the rowan tree. The child would be gone soon.

She moved across the barren towards the heart. The ground was hard and hot under her feet. This forest was real somewhere outside the Dreaming. She must make the journey in both places, in the same seasons. She read the stars above her. The air smelled of lightning, smoke, and smolder. Thin rivers of heat flowed through the rowan's roots just beneath her feet. She felt them like veins under the skin, her skin. She called the earth through her and released thunder into the clear night. The wind of a thousand wigs fled to the outer circles of Arden. The forest floor appeared to ripple with scurrying paws and hooves through the litter. Even the ash jumped from the child's skin, dislodged as the earth ran through it. White-hot lightning crackled from the branches. Fissures in the trunk reveal embers within. She reached out and let the flames consume her.

The owl watched the child place its hand on the trunk. It answered the question without words. Flames shot into the sky as the phoenix was released from its core. The heart of Arden reborn from ashes.

Cousin in Florida
by John Grey

You say it's just a phony menace,
these alligators on the banks of
the backyard stream, slowly warming
their somber blood in late afternoon sunshine
We are as safe as if they were butterflies
or deer or even children splashing
in that slow curdle of water.
There is enough fish in that muddy current
to feed an entire planet of reptiles.
There's no risk of one slipping up
to the house in the dead of night,
dragging a sleeping body in its mouth
down to a hollow in the banks
for later feasting.
On and on you rattle, as if to convince
yourself as much as me.
I listen to you
while staring at these scaly beasts,
horrified but fascinated
as one unzips an eye,
slowly stretches open its chain saw jaw.
That mouth is too narrow
to take all of me in
but it sure is wide enough
to chew on the flesh,
spit out the bones,
of that story of yours.

Marport
by Zuriel van Belle

Marport is an island nearby. During the most recent Marport Materiality Review, 100% of respondents did not recall having heard of the island. When polled, visitors to the island do sometimes recall its existence. Marport, if one can recall it, is suitable for a day trip.

Visit Marport by taking the ferry. It leaves the city every day at 8 am and returns at 6 pm. From the Marport Port, visitors can take the island's premier and only bus line, the 27, to any of its eleven stops.

A place for birdwatchers, Marport boasts many species of seabirds:

Western Gulls
Thayer's Gulls
Sabine's Gulls
Ring-billed Gulls
Mew Gulls
Iceland Gulls
Herring Gulls
Heermann's Gulls
Glaucous-winged Gulls
Glaucous Gulls
Franklin's Gulls
California Gulls
Bonaparte's Gulls
Black-legged Kittiwakes

From the shore, if misty clouds allow it, you can see the raised hump of the old deck bridge in the middle of the sea. The Henry Prospect Bridge was spearheaded by Marport's 12th mayor and *heir-at-law* to the Murphy Potato Chip Company on the south side of the island.

Murphy Potato Chip Company proudly grows all of their potatoes on Marport using the Marport Zig Zag Planting Method®. The zig-zag planting technique was developed to protect against the highly localized earthquakes known to occur in the area. Murphy Potato Chip Company has four flavors of potato chips: regular, unsalted, salted, and classic. When given the choice, the birds on the shore choose classic.

In recent years, the birds have perched on the railings of the old deck bridge, which, at low tide, lie submerged two centimeters under the sea's surface. The gulls levitate on the two miles of submerged railing and avoid completely the small exposed hump of the bridge.

An unpredicted, though quite predictable flood, turned the once-peninsula of Marport into an island. The bridge, built to reconnect Marport with the city, was submerged in a truly unpredictable flood 29 days after its completion and 2 days before its grand opening.

The rain that drowned the bridge was Marport's last recorded rainfall; however, rain gear is recommended, as the weather is generally cloudy and always threatens rain. Umbrellas are available for purchase in the Marport Port Gift Shop (open from 6 to 8 am).

Venture just inland from the port to Oak Park, a destination for visitors. Oak Park was home to a small introduced population of house sparrows, a biodiversity project promoted by the island's 17th mayor. Unfortunately, the sparrows vacated Marport shortly after their introduction. Fortunately, mew gulls frequent Oak Park and are available for photos.

Should you remember to visit Marport, you may recall that it is an island nearby.

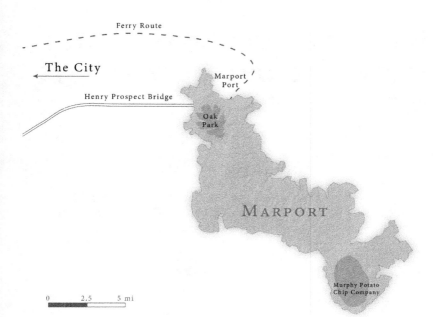

We May Never Remove Our Masks around the Monkeys
by Arnold B. Cabdriver

'One of us must remove our mask to lure the monkey.'

'But who of us will lure the monkey?'

We drew straws. First the woman in the antelope mask. Next the boy in the elephant mask. The man who made the rounds passing straws wore the mask of the jackdaw.

'As you can see I've made a web of finest chain as thin as a spiders' web.'

He shined a light to the corners. The threads sparkled.

'But what if we too are trapped in the net?'

He held up a knife.

'You all have knives,' he said. 'Defend yourselves.'

'But if we knife the monkey?'

'We will use him as lure for a second monkey.'

'And if we knife the second monkey?'

'Of course we will have a third monkey to contend with.'

'And if the third is knifed?'

'Knife again.'

'And if the fourth? And the fifth? And the sixth?'

We sweated.

'Then, little by little,' he said, 'we will have destroyed all anonymity.'

Hospital for Reanimated Pets
by Kellye McBride

In hindsight, this was probably not the best place for a teachable moment about death with my eleven-year-old.

The whole thing had been Abby's idea in the first place. "I can't let her go," she had said. "Please dad." Osiris was our thirteen-year-old ragdoll cat my wife Olivia adopted right before we started dating. Yesterday, we found him hiding under the back patio after he refused to eat or drink for several days. I was bracing myself to have that time-old conversation between parent and child, but then Abby remembered something she had heard about from a friend from school, a pet hospital off the interstate that revived sick or recently deceased animals. She begged me to go, telling me all the way about her friend's cat who turned out alive and healthy. I decided this time I would be the "cool" dad and keep my mouth shut. After all, how much trouble could it be?

As we sat in the dimly lit waiting room, we watched as sobbing, hysterical pet owners came in with shoeboxes and plastic crates, only to receive newly re-animated hamsters or dogs with glowing white eyes.

"Do you think Osiris will look like that once he's finished?" Abby asked, nudging me. He was currently nestled in his cat carrier on Abby's lap while we waited to be called.

"I guess," was all I could definitively say. When I was Abby's age, my father didn't even have the sense to make up a story about a farm. He just informed me my black lab had been hit by a semi-truck over breakfast one morning and that I better not make a huge fuss. Even though I still resented him years later, I'm wondering now if I could have done a better job.

"First time?" the older woman next to us asked. She was

wearing a juvenile pastel cat-print sweater and matching earrings that suggested she was not mentally playing with a full deck.

"Yeah," I said. "How could you tell?"

The woman smiled toothlessly and gazed down at the empty carrier by her feet. "This is my seventh. I didn't know what I would do if I had to part with any of my precious little angels."

As a parent, I live in constant fear about the values I'm imparting on my children. Looking at this woman, as she pulled out her phone to show me and Abby photos of all of her "precious little angels" with glowing white eyes and claws dressed in various outfits, I was reconsidering whether letting my daughter re-animate our family cat was a good idea.

"Lindstrom?" a veterinary nurse called out.

"That's me. Best of luck!" the woman said, hurrying toward the front desk where a hissing tabby was waiting for her.

I picked up some of the waiting room literature lying around that explained the details of the miracle procedure. The dying or dead animal would be taken out behind the pet hospital to a special area. The pet would be buried there for two hours, after which the pet would emerge and be brought back to its owner. The brochure indicated that the re-animation had something to do with the soil underneath the hospital. The hospital staff still weren't sure exactly *why* it worked, only *how*. Once an animal was buried there, it would come back stronger, healthier, and more *alive* than before.

"Wow, I wonder what this thing is built on, some kind of Native American burial ground?"

Abby rolled her eyes. "Dad, that's racist."

Last month Abby admonished me and Olivia over the fact that we called Indigenous Peoples' Day "Columbus Day" out of ignorance. Still, it's a strange feeling when the small, helpless being that you helped bring into the world suddenly surpasses you in your own knowledge of it.

"Sorry honey, you're right."

In our family, we had a system. Olivia handled all conversations about menstruation, boys, and anything involving a Wonderbra. Meanwhile, I agreed that I would cover changing a flat tire and the cruel reality that our life on Earth is both fleeting and short. However, I was starting to think that Olivia got the better deal. I wanted to tell Abby so many things and also shield her from them as long as I possibly could. Yet she was also a lot smarter than I ever was. What could I tell her that (I suspected) she didn't already know? Is this what fatherhood is, trying the best you can in your own, imperfect way before you fade into irrelevance?

"Dad!" Abby said sharply. I realized I must have been dozing off, as she was standing by the nurses' station with Osiris. "They're ready for us."

"Coming," I said, letting the brochure fall out of my lap.

"Dad, Osiris keeps biting me."

I heard Osiris's low-level growls all the way from the front seat, even with volume on the satellite radio cranked up high. It was unlike him, he had always been a mellow cat.

"Sweetie, you probably should stop reaching back there," I said, fiddling with the dial. "He's just been brought back to life, I can't imagine the kind of stress he is under."

"Don't you think he seems different somehow?"

"Well, I mean he's got white eyes for starters."

"No, not that. I feel like he's a completely different cat."

We came to a stoplight. It had started to rain outside and I turned the wipers on. We both watched the water for a few minutes as it swirled into the storm drain.

"Honey, when I was your age I had a black lab named Thunder. Did I ever tell you this story?"

Abby looked down in her lap. "Yeah, that your dad just came in one morning and said he got run over like nothing happened."

"Yup. I was pretty upset," the light changed and we merged into traffic. The rain switched from a light sprinkle to a steady downpour. "I always thought he did that because he was a cold-hearted jackass, but looking back on it now I think he was trying to teach me something, in his own way."

"What's that?"

"Sometimes letting go is the best solution."

Abby looked back at Osiris, who hissed and yowled at her while clawing at his cage, and then back at me. In that moment, I saw a trace of the little girl who had to hold my hand while crossing the street because she was too scared.

"Dad, could you…?" was all she had to say. I turned off the next exit that took us to a country road and out into a pasture. I pulled over, put the car in park, and took the carrier from the backseat, avoiding Osiris's claws.

"Want me to do the honors?" I asked. Abby nodded, wiping her face with the sleeve of her sweatshirt.

I walked ten paces into the field, smelling of mud and cow manure. I would have to explain to Olivia why my jeans and shoes were soaked, but that didn't matter. I set the carrier down in the field and pulled the little door up. Osiris shot out of the carrier like a cannon, hissing because the field was so wet. In the distance, I saw a little farmhouse with a barn and a wispy column of smoke coming out of the chimney. I could hear the distant clucking of chickens and the sound of tires squelching on the back roads. I waited for a moment longer, listening to the engine hum before I picked up the carrier, tossed it in the back and got back in the driver's seat. Abby was staring at her hands, tears streaming down her cheeks.

"I'm an idiot," she said, sobbing. I put my hand on her arm. "I should have just let him go in the first place."

"No, honey. You're human."

The Duck
by Eric Thralby

The night of a storm, a duck banged into the window.

That's Quackers, my daughter said.

Rain fell onto the window. Branches tapped the walls.

I came to the window. There was the duck in the mud on its back. It did not move like a duck, but like meat bewitched.

That's my duck, she said. I love my duck.

I dressed in a number of shirts and rubber gloves and entered into the ripping and tearing of the storm. Here was the duck in the mud. It opened and closed its bill. It reached away from me and dragged itself with its wing, which was broken. I scooped the duck up.

My daughter banged on the window. She smiled and showed Bemelmans.

Should I have brought him up close to the glass and waved with his little webbed foot?

She opened the book.

Even through the glass and in the storm, I heard her voice come through very faintly, reciting the lines I had read her and read her, as if she were now reading it herself.

In an old house in Paris that was covered with vines

Lived twelve little girls in two straight lines

The duck moved its wings around in my arms. It felt like a vase I had hoped would stay glued.

In two straight lines they broke their bread

And brushed their teeth and went to bed

Rain streamed down the duck and I felt its heart beat into my thumb. I moved my fingers over its throat like a ripe ear of corn.

They left the house at half past nine

In two straight lines in rain or shine

It went limp in my arms like an unfolded shirt.

    note: I am not a father. This piece is false. I do not know what to say to a child when an animal dies, but I suspect it is a moment which reminds you to live very fiercely. Once I tended to a raccoon which was injured in our yard. We had a sliding glass door and there the raccoon lay. I could not see if it was external, internal or age. Raccoons have a great deal of beautiful fur. It arrived one day as I was leaving for school. I brought it a jar lid full of water. It did not drink. It did not move from the doormat. When I returned from school I brought it a second jar lid full of Cheerios. As I went to sleep that night, I listened to it breathing. And around six in the morning, as it had become very loud, I went to the sliding glass door. The raccoon sat up as if trying to reach something. It growled or purred, as if its chest were rumbling, then reaching further and further, it shrieked, unrolled and then lay very flat. I buried the raccoon with the doormat, the jar lids and a small handful of roses.

A Small Group of Fishermen
by Arnold B. Cabdriver

A small group of fishermen tend a dock. The fishermen know everything that goes on in our town. The fishermen sit around skinning fish, and dwelling on Benjamin Carson. It's not right that a boy is born so awful, says the first fisherman, holding a knife in the eyes of a fish. The second fisherman, his hands round as melons, is silent. The third fisherman says, I do not know whether he is worse, or whether she is worse having birthed him.

Not far from the fisherman, a boy runs through the rain. He has told his school companions that in a terrible storm there are mermaids which come up shirtless from the sea. He is going to take one and do everything he wants with her. His companions run close behind him, their clothing soaked and looking more like second skin.

They reach the dock where it reeks like nets of fish.

I'm going to put my willy into her, the boy says.

If you do, says another, she'll yank it off. That's what mermaids do to sailors.

The sea is a black-grey, as if the rain has beaten all of the green to the bottom.

The boys strip naked. They are all going to put their willies into a mermaid. They jump into the water. Their bodies invisible inside the thickness of the ocean. Their heads like small lanterns in the unfathomable darkness.

Fishermen deliver terrible things from the ocean, things which were never meant to be seen or eaten. But such is the nature of fishermen.

The three fishermen stood very close to the door when Mrs. Carson opened after their pounding. They spilled immediately inside.

He was caught in the rain. He has changed, they said, the immense storm behind them.

The boy tries to jump from their arms. They rush with Mrs. Carson into the bathroom where she breaks open the bath.

The fishermen lower Benjamin Carson into the water. He has turned purple around his eyes. His neck was swollen. He flopped his legs in the bath and grabbed at his mother.

He tried to touch her but had little control of his arms, as his body was kicking and slamming to breathe.

They did not want to hold her back, but her nose had started to bleed.

When the water closed over his mouth, Ben became calm.

His eyes lost all blueness and became two black marbles. His hair drifted in the bathwater like weeds. His skin had begun to gleam.

Two fishermen stayed stooped low beside the tub. The third stood and explained that Ben can no longer survive outside water. He will have to be taken away.

The fishermen took Ben in their arms. His skin had become more slick and his spine more flexible. It took all three to get Ben into the storm but when he felt the rain he became calm again and lay draped in the first fisherman's arms.

Two of Ben's comrades ran up to the fisherman. Is that Ben? Is he hurt?

He will not be the same, the fishermen said.

The boys stopped in the street. They wore bright yellow slickers. And as the boys faded under the storm, more neighbors came through. A crowd grew on their way to the harbor, then creaked onto the pier while the fishermen carried the boy to the edge.

We know what it means, begins the first fisherman, for a boy to be taken. He regards the water seeping into Ben's neck. We know, begins the third fisherman, Ben Carson has disappointed us all. But see his calmness. See his eyes as he departs from us forever. The second fisherman turns to the crowd and shows them the boy. Seemingly he means by this, We will all meet our fate.

We prayed for Benjamin Carson.

Then the fishermen turned to the edge of the pier and lowered Ben into the ocean. He sank at first, like a waterlogged branch. Down and down, until he disappeared.

Until there was nothing, only rain hitting water.

We crowded the fishermen. Could we have done anything different? Could we have stopped him somehow?

But we could not move them. They hung their heads, as deaf as rocks.

It was then that the hands emerged, webbed and brilliantly glowing. Though now drawn back to the body, stunted and delicate, paddling lightly up. Then it broke the surface. The creature regarded us, from the fishermen, to the comrades, but Benjamin's mother was not there. She sat alone in the house, which she had shared with her son. I, it said, but could not say anymore.

The creature swam away into the dark water and over time the crowd dispersed. But when all had gone home, the fishermen stirred. A boat light clicked on. And their schooner rattled to life. They crept out from the harbor and lumbered out toward the ocean, lowering their nets.

Meow
by Jonathan van Belle

Fox Paolo and Fox Francesca sidewinding up the coop,
Tossing their sashes in the grass, under woody smooth breeze-blowing dusk.
Full moon of heavy feeding, jammy scoops;
Lop-eared hiccups in chicken lipstick of chicky juice.

We William-Tell-Overture off with a coiled rattlesnake shot!
I, you, hunt the koklass and quail and puritans and fox martyrs;
Our fangs splash a fizzy-dizzy demi-sec up and down;
Our puffing like one lung drowning and our horses huffing, hissing, kiffing.

Foxes off waltzing, fiddling, gobbling sponge cake, frosted dove, duck breast.
I love, I love the quacking pillows, muskets, mounted soldiers,
Fevers, heels, varnish, oomph, diamond-makers, divers
Kicking the waves seismic.

Spring's cherry-wreathed fauns from wet tree limbs chirrup:
"Pollen, please, in every climate!
Tiers of rose-stuffed swans!
Piñatas of chocolate-covered bluebird hearts!"

I, you, meowing,
Guzzled as the titmouse does a wiggly wasp
In duet of bodies mixed up and off.
Ave landica, gratia plena! The hounds are hot!

I, you, Rossini, Mozart, Offenbach, in rabbit fur, fragranced, in reindeer antlers
Bucking, hamming, bellydancing from Acapulco to Wool-loomooloo
On teacup tippy-toes, meowing
Below a naked man nailed to the mistletoe.

Dripping drum and galloping gulp and ultraviolet mouth
Peckish come to bite as a blush, as a burning church, into our plum;

Roost on us, rebellious bird, clawing hawk, twitchy twirler.
Siren, let the sourpusses see us sinning.

Bury our merlot sparrow spasms in bubbly bathoms.
With honeyed thyrsus whip off the monkish! Faster!
A taut, blasty quake and away the drainer, violator, diminisher, criticaster.
Howl and meow to Joy, my rose hip and Achelois.

You Don't Say - Fabrice Poussin

Rescue
by Desiree Ducharme

Kenya made space in my heart for love. Before her, there was only me and vague words. We think about hearts being a specific size or shape. In fact, they are intentionally flexible by design. They have a purpose. They hold space within us. We condition them to extend our lives. If you've loved unconditionally, you understand why this organ is kept in a vulnerable bone-cage at our core. The brain is locked down. The skull is solid with holes for your senses. The organized filters through which our mind processes the data of life. It is a shield to keep things away from the delicate tissue of the brain. The smallest bump or bruise to our grey-matter can be fatal. The heart is built for living. We are constantly trying to push it beyond its limits. Its shield is open in places. Intentionally reckless and challenging. There are holes and chambers for rushing into and out of. The heart intends to beat and be beaten. It rattles and rails against its enclosure. It pulls and pushes the essence of us. It provides the tides for the oceans within. Before Kenya, there was no tide within me. She was the missing moon.

I never wanted a dog. T did, it was on The List, right after "Move-in Together" and just before "Get Married." So, he went and got a puppy. He gifted it to me so we could share the experience. The only living things you should gift are plants and yeast. Life cannot be given. It can be lived. It can be shared. It can be ended. Life belongs to those who live. You cannot gift it. Sativa, the gift-dog, was part of T's life plan. Like all living things, the dog didn't follow the plan, it was busy being a puppy. The gift-dog chewed his favorite shoes, his wallet, the couch, the book titled "Don't Shoot the Dog." T considered the gift-dog as mine so I was to blame. I was not consistent with the training. Sativa ate the book before I could read it. You can't control the lives or actions of others, even if you love them. Sativa was his own being. I respected his boundaries and put my shoes and important things where he couldn't reach them. Kenya did the same. She held him accountable for his behavior when she witnessed it. She encouraged delinquency when needed. We gave each other space. This worked for us.

My "I'm-leaving-thanks-for-the-life-experience" note was in the Birkenstocks I'd given T for his Birthday. After Sativa chewed his pair to unrecognizable pieces in March, he almost took him to the pound. This life he'd gifted to me was disposable. Ironic when you consider I was only allowed 3 squares of TP, "For the environment!" T was big on keeping score for the environment. He weaponized gift giving by adding an 'experience' to every gift. T's gift for my 22nd birthday was a trip to his college friend's wedding. I was gifted the experience of being quiet and looking pretty in Texas. On T's birthday, I had to work but when I got home I woke him up and gave him the shoes. The guilt that flashed in his eyes told me he'd already been sleeping with who ever she was. We experienced irreconcilable differences after that. It was leaving Kenya that broke me. She was not on any list but once I knew her, I loved her. My heart was flooded with her. I didn't know what to do with that but I could not stay and I could not take her. She would be fine without me. I would not. I made it work with T for two more years.

Kenya chose me. All of me. From my cold toes to morning-breath to three-day-old still-wet hair, she never shied away. She was always a yes to adventure or staying in. Kenya never told me to smile and was always game for a good cry or howling. She preferred howling outside and never missed an opportunity to indulge in her primal, canid urges. She never missed an opportunity to run. I'm a terrible runner, so I gave her space to run. She always came back when I called, in her own time. We spent hours howling at each other in the forests and across the deserts of the southwest. Almost as many hours as we spent gently humming to each other or singing along with the radio. Kenya learned to sing from the whales off the California coast. She was a terrible swimmer so she sang whale songs. I always came back to shore, in my own time. She made sacrifices to stay with me as well. Sativa ran off the spring T and I finally called it quits. Kenya went into witness-protection. I hid her from him. I did it for me. I did it for the stretchmarks on my heart. In the fall, Kenya and I started over and were together as much as possible. Sometimes life's a bitch and sometimes bitches need to reclaim their lives.

    Kenya had been abandoned on a beach near Del Mar. She had a name tag and hungry eyes. She came into my life like the evening tide, slowly and inevitably. She shaped my heart. I was in the waves with T. I didn't realize it was time to leave until all our stuff was wet. I wasn't mad. You can't be mad at the tide anymore than you can hold a grudge with the sun for setting. The tide was in, your stuff is wet, the sun has set. This is Kenya. Life is forever better. You don't think about the tide receding. You don't consider the tide may never come in again. You just become accustomed to the musty smell of wet dog and the sound of contented sighs from the foot of your bed. You cannot plan a rescue but if you're lucky you find you are a part of one.

Dytiscus Larvae: a Dramatic Scene
by Yuan Changming

One most ferocious robber in the pond
World, observes a zoologist, is a slim,
Streamlined insect called the Dytiscus larvae:
Lying in ambush on a water grass
He suddenly shoots at lightning speed
To his prey (or anything moving or smelling
Of 'animal' in any way, a fat tadpole, for
Instance), darts underneath it, then quickly
Jerks up his head, grabs it in his jaws
Injects his poisonous glandular secretion into it
Dissolves its entire inside into a liquid soup
And sucks as it swells up first, and then gradually
Shrinks to a limp bundle of skin until it finally falls
From his fatal kiss. Very few animals

According to the observer
Even when starved to death would attack
Let alone eat an equal-sized animal
Of their own species

But the Dytiscus does, just as man does
Within or without a pond

Black Bird
by Ariel Kusby

I cannot stand your velvet cloak that holds
the dark in. Unprepared, I stayed

with you until the wind spoke of mothers and I remembered
my own smell. Every day I checked the solidness

of skin, the speed of blood, the shape of eyes
against the rain. I know you watched

my living rituals, the imitation light I held up to my face
to push you out. Anything to keep

from growing feathers and spreading out into the winter.
We are not unalike, black bird. You know I cannot bear to hear

a heartbeat. I will not call you by your name.
Spring is rising, summoning you and your daughters.

Black bird, I've given you everything I can. Let me play
my breathing games. I am wanted

by yellowing strands of light. Don't worry, black bird:
I'll save my heat until your return.

The Cormorant
by Sarah Bartlett

"Thence up he flew, and on the Tree of Life, / The middle tree and highest there that grew, / Sat like a cormorant."
                                                    - John Milton

The cormorant finds me walking alone
and dives right in
takes over my left ventricle
and changes my blood into salt water
I feel held for the first time
a gentle brining of the tongue
Inside me the cormorant washes itself
My heart an old kitchen
a place for banging and scraps
The beach where I stand a cook
a set of arms for the dead
We can never arrange ourselves
this way and achieve such beauty
These whorls and hollows
are not made by the Internet
They are just made then
left behind like mothers

The cormorant likes things
melancholy and public
its lips arriving triumphantly
on the outside of me
crushed word remnants of
honey and squid drip
It doesn't care that we are all scared
We are all so scared
I Google "what death feels like" and
"shrimp stir fry" in quick succession
The cormorant creates a new typography
writes about me in my diary
She craves happiness
It's too easy to break this thing
The branch under me

the granddaughter of the branch under me
No one remembers how we landed here
When it climbs out of me
both of us cry

The wind flings into every orifice
clocking speeds like a rabbit
and fucking and fucking
I'm afraid of losing myself
the cormorant finding a new perch
my body finally broken by release
The beach is full of strangers and dogs
The cormorant preens and hides
and flaps back out like a deer's tongue
ocean air a salt lick
There are three different kinds of tears
like snowflakes they individuate under glass

When I pray the cormorant answers
God is right here and we are fake safe
our bodies laced into the sand's patchwork kingdom
the same thing written over and over
with the end of a stick
Our private nomenclature appears on the Internet
with new hashtags and thousands of views
Memory now a permanent instrument
outside the body
I run to make my lungs remember
They are lonely
it's hard to hold the power cord to language
I let them scream
The cormorant screams
there is no one here to say who is louder

I walk inside other people's footprints
I shrink my stride to make them fit
put hearts at the end of sentences
like stamps and hit send
I look inside a window
of a shingled cottage behind a dune
interior sweet as a doll's house
my face in the mirror over the dresser
I put it on the Internet as proof

I'm relieved everyone can see
the real me
The cormorant is so thrilled
it sends a text of the image of the image
of my face to a friend as a reminder
We keep walking
I forget myself
I look at my phone
Sand rearranges its symmetry
waits like the top of a throat
The cormorant is also hungry

Pain is a message
ropes of electric flesh
pulled tight until the face reacts
Under glass things become clearer
breadcrumbs building
toward something true
I blink
The cormorant blinks
we press the hatchet of our body
against the wind
Shells decorate the ground
We write our names in the sand
because the tide is coming in
We gift ourselves folded gently
into its mouth

Frog Calls
by Yuan Changming

The frog has stopped calling
In the early light, but I
Still feel the sound waves
Surging towards my mind's shore
Though different from the frogs
My mother used to listen to when
I must have heard deep
Inside her teenager womb
As she walked at dusk from her first job
In town back to her native village

Their calls separate us into two worlds
And my nostalgia is her nostalgia
Echoing from generation to another
As loud as the song of the heart
From the long lost rice fields

Fireflies
by Z.B. Wagman

"The fireflies came out tonight. It's the first time I've seen them in a while. I know how much you like them." His voice hummed like the softest of sandpaper against her skin. "There weren't that many of them. Only a couple of pairs. Still, they were like tiny stars floating off into the night."

She could feel him close to her. It was the way the air moved in the room around him, like static clinging to him. She could almost feel her breath being drawn out of her chest towards him, her lungs too weak to put up much of a fight. "Fairy lights," she said in that rasping voice that could only remind her of her mother's in the last years of her life.

"Yes, like fairy lights," he agreed. She hated when he did that--agree with her just because she was old. He was treating her like a child. But she was still in here. She needed him to know that she was still in here. She labored upward, reaching towards where she thought he was. She wanted to scream at him. To let him know that she was still alive.

But all that came from her struggle was a rasping cough.

"Careful mom, save your breath." His hand caught hers. He was so much stronger than she remembered. She could feel his arm around her, lowering her back into bed.

The mood passed. He was still holding her hand. She liked it when he did that. It was one of the only ways she knew that he was actually there. The fog had stolen his face from her, as well as those memories. Only when he held her hand did she remember him as the little boy she once knew.

"Tell me more about the stars," she asked, wanting to keep him near her for a little while longer.

"Yes, mom," he said and she could hear the smile in his voice. "They were awful pretty tonight. I took the kids down to the walnut fields--you remember how much I loved them when I was younger?--and we played tag well after dark. Jacob saw his first shooting star. And it was like the whole world made sense in that one moment. Such wonder. Was I ever that young? It feels like another lifetime..."

She could feel the tide sweeping him away from her. She wanted so desperately to hear the end of the story. She grasped his hand as tight as her aged muscles could but she couldn't hold on. His words blurred into susurration of the tides.

When the story was done the man sat, clutching his mother's hand in both of his. Tears ran freely down his face. He did not try to wipe them away. Slowly, with the care he had afforded his son even before his first step, he laid his mother's arm at her side and closed her eyes.

The Bone
by Michal Goldstein

there is no greater image of
desperation
than the dog that runs back for
the bone
for the twentieth time
on a lonely afternoon.

it returns home to its master
lays down at his feet
sets down the emblem of his
dedication
and the master laughs,
accepts his gift half-heartedly
sheds enough love to last until
the next round
and then sends the dog back
to fetch.

i don't think i'm the dog—
i think i'm the bone
tossed around and used
but still,
thinking it's nice
to be needed.

dropped at your feet, me, and
you, for what it's worth,
take me in with one arm
warm me to the touch
then throw me back into
cold air.

the sky watches in
anticipation
the dog
hardly notices
and you, for what it's worth,
don't notice either.

66 *Menagerie, shop window, Paris - Roger Camp*

Blackberry Epiphany
by Michael Baldwin

Venturing fingers among the tangle
of blackberry thorn canes,
questing their dark elusive prize,
plucking each plump bundle, then
easing it from the labyrinth
of defending claws, I discover
one gleaming berry ridden by a petite
beetle, her flat, yellow shield
an extravagant contrast against
the obsidian fruit's glistening bulb.

Elegy to the Great Auk
by Yuan Changming

Eldey Island. 3 July 1844. Two Iceland fishermen
Caught and killed two birds, while a third used
His boots to tread their half-hatched egg into pieces

That's the inhuman end of a whole species used to be
Called Penguin. The feathered couple was much
More loyal to each other than any human marriage
Their kind had survived last ice age, flying gracefully

Everywhere, in particular along Newfoundland coasts
Helping sailors to escape from dangers, but now they
Are totally forgotten, except in a little poem like this

Hummingbird
by G Michael Smith

the sky was there
distorted at the edges
but there
clear crystal blue

his wings burned
his mind locked
he battled the Plexiglas sky

over and again
his head bumped
hoping
for an improbable escape

I was afraid
his death
would stain my hands
like black pitch

I saw his obsession
lying to his wings
each invisible beat
bringing him closer

his truth needed to be told
the sky needed to lie

it was up to me
to eclipse the sun

transform
his reality
to a phosphorescent bullet
shooting out
into a summer day

70 *Nice Place - Fabrice Poussin*

Gongxifacai [恭喜发财]: An Idiomatic Chinese Calendar
by Yuan Changming

Rats abandon a sinking ship
Cows have no business in horseplay
Tigers die and leave their skins
If you chase two rabbits, you will not catch either one

Noble dragons don't have friends
Snakes follow the way of serpents
A horse may stumble though he has four legs
A goat owned by two people sleeps outside

The higher a monkey climbs, the more he shows his behind
Rooster today, feather duster tomorrow
Dogs that bark much don't bite
A pig's tail will never make a good arrow

Or Was it Not a Koi
by Sarah Bartlett

Slow pearl body
A gleam under water
Even the dog pauses
To consider that
You are alive
Now you are alive
Moving in slow circles
Around the pond
And we are alive watching
You in your ignorant beauty
Exist so hard
The trees bend down
And elsewhere the ocean
Pulls itself toward your
Glow in the park's sink
Where sickness is nowhere near
Your milky scales
That gather light into some
Kind of celestial afterthought
And elsewhere the pandemic
Blooms and rearranges
Our faces into ghost faces
And like ghosts we float
Like you we rise up through
The night's surface and disappear
Into new constellations

Cat for Cole
by Mickey Collins

"We should get a cat for Cole," said Brad to Alice. "A pet would do him some good."

Alice looked to Brad from behind her "#1 Mom" coffee cup. She pulled the muffin he was about to grab away from him. "Remember what the doctor said?"

Brad's face fell, but he nodded. Alice returned to catching up on the latest headlines on her phone. Brad counted the seconds in his head, waiting for Alice to return to his question, but she didn't. He weighed his options as if deciding whether to drop an atom bomb or not. During these weekend mornings, she was usually in the best mood. To bring it up later would only be dragging it on, and Alice hated that. He pushed his luck again. "Anyway," he began.

"Anyway," Alice cut him off. She didn't take her eyes off her phone as she tore pieces from the blueberry muffin. "A cat would mean more work for me. Who would have to take care of it? To clean up its messes? To feed it and clean its poop? Certainly not a 4 year-old boy. And definitely not you who's always either at work or in front of the TV."

"Cole needs a friend. He would learn responsibility in time. A cat would teach him compassion and about living things."

Alice chewed on her muffin. "What about a fish?"

"Can we compromise on a catfish?"

Alice let out a laugh. She couldn't help herself when it came to his dumb sense of humor. "Maybe a *gold*fish."

"What do you think, I'm made of money?"

Alice laughed louder now. She set her phone down as

Cole made his way into the kitchen, rubbing the sleep from his eyes. "Hi honey, ready for breakfast?"

Cole gave a slow nod. He hopped up onto the chair next to Brad as Alice got up to make him cereal.

"Hey pal," said Brad. He tousled Cole's sandy brown hair. "Do you want to go to the pet store today?"

Cole's eyes opened wide as he nodded vigorously.

"What do you think about a goldfish?" asked Brad.

Cole shook his head.

"Well, what kind of fish would you want?" asked Alice as she set the bowl of cereal down in front of Cole.

Cole didn't have to think very long. "I want a spider!"

Brad and Alice looked at each other in surprise. In unison they said, "No."

"I want a spider!" said Cole.

"What about a cat?" asked Alice. "You can name him Spider."

Cole gave the matter serious thought before replying, "Ok."

Brad gave Alice a sly smile. She rolled her eyes at him.

Saved by Cats
by AJD

Curled into a ball on the bed.
Better off dead. Better off dead.
Relentless mantra in my head.
Better off dead. Better off dead.

Turn on back and before my eyes,
life's report card flashes by,
a bottomless column of F and I.
Better off dead. Better off dead.
Too tired to cry. Too sick for why.

How should I do it, though I never would?
How could I do it? I feel I should.
Better off dead. Better off dead.
Unlike lost pals, with gun and poison,
a rope or blade, my preferred options.

Whispers hoarse in befouling pall,
I plot the options on shadowed wall.
Better off dead. Better off dead.
Pondering when, when will I die?
I see the future, a very short ride.
Just... frothy breath or ebbing tide?

Curled into a ball on the bed.
Better off... Cats interrupt, feed me, feed me.
I protest with venum, leave me, leave me.
They pounce and fall, swatting air, racing over, on a tear.
I kick them off, suffer cries, wrankled hair, sullen stares.

Curled into a ball on... Flashing talon slashes skin,
pointed fang pierces vein.
I thrash, convulse, hide in sheets,
another stain, marking pain.
Enough! I howl.
Paws skitter, then a silence.
Lifting odorous veil, I spot a casual licking,
at the door, leading out.

Saved by cats.

The Golden Brown Dog
by Nicholas Yandell

The golden brown dog,
Lies on the golden brown floor,
Not just blending in,
But becoming one,
With the transitional path,
Of the comings and goings,
Of civilization around him.

He takes comfort,
In the close proximity,
Of a black bicycle,
And the liberation,
Its wheels might bring,
To otherwise,
More reliably,
Stationary,
Bodies.

He hears,
Its clangorous bell,
As a beckoning of freedom,
To his golden brown form,
Lying there,
Fur gently bristling,
From a light window breeze,
Like a wheat field,
Bending,
Helplessly,
To the whims of the wind.

Black Birds in the Backyard
by Lynette G. Esposito

Under a canopy of blue sky
A light breeze lifts the new leaves on summer trees.
Flocks of blackbirds season the backyard
Like pepper cloves sprinkled randomly
on a green earth.

A flurry, a swirl charging the mix to flight.
and silence falls as if they were never there.

My Cat
by George White

My cat brings me gravel. He picks it up from the drive just outside and brings it to the kitchen. His catches tinkle as they are dropped on the tiles and my cat looks up and smiles.

He is pleased to offer me such a grand present, I can tell. Each droplet of gravel he brings me is a soft shade of grey, cream, or brown. Tiny on the floor but large in his mouth.

I have learned to do a morning scan for these prizes left on my floor. Too many times have I been rudely dragged from my sleepy morning state to sharp pieces of rock cutting through the tough skin on my feet. Waking up is hard enough without an injury to accompany it.

My fellow cat owners offer me their traumatic stories of poor dead (or worse, dying) creatures that their predators bring them. They say my cat will soon be doing the same. It is their nature.

I'm not so sure. My cat is older now and much more agile than the silly kitten I first brought home. Yet, no poor defenceless mouse has been dropped to my kitchen tiles. Just the gravel. Everyday.

Maybe my cat, like me, enjoys the home comforts. Why go further when he can bring me perfect little gifts just from the drive?

We curl up in front of the T.V. together with the heating on. Occasionally, my cat will stand to stretch every vertebra in his back, and it inspires me to do the same. A click often accompanies as I do so, it creates space for comfort.

My cat will get up unannounced and leap out of the cat flap with a flick of his thin white tail. I am left with a warm spot at the end of the sofa to stretch my toes into.

I will often sit and watch and wait until he returns with cheeks full like a hamster. My cat will walk proudly past me and make his way into the kitchen and I hear the tinkling of the gravel on my tiles again.

The ringing is my summon so I quickly attend. There, lying on his side, is my silly cat, batting gravel from one paw to another. His gifts.

Pig & Cat - Roger Camp

Story of Sabi
by Heather Glover

Sabi wandered through the long grasses, skirting around enormous trees that gave plenty of shade and even better cover from predators. Her mother had taught her long ago not to meander out in the open or you may find yourself soaring above the clouds on the way to someone's dinner table. In fact, it was common practice in the whole colony to use birds as a threat when small ones were not doing what they were told. Not eating your clover? An owl will eat you. Don't want to sweep your shed fur out of the den? A hawk will make you its dinner.

Quite frankly, Sabi thought that the realistic threat of predators was scary enough without added child nightmares attached, thank you very much.

The small mouse kept her ears pricked and her nose scented to the wind, all senses on high alert. She had never gone this far from the nest on her own before, but her mother had decided she was old enough to be sent on her first assignment: gathering wild dandelion seeds to store for winter. Sabi had been so excited to be given such an important task she had nearly burst with pride, grabbing one of the small baskets and rushing towards the den entrance. However her mother had stopped her before she could go out into the day. Sabi remembered her lecture exactly.

"Make sure to check both ways before crossing any paths. Predators usually don't hunt in the middle of the day but you never know with snakes and the odd weasel. Keep your ears alert and your eyes open and check the branches above every once in a while to make sure no birds are sneaking up on you. Robins and other songbirds aren't overly dangerous, just aggressive, but if you see a hawk dive into the nearest hole and stay there until it moves on."

Talk about overloading and petrifying a young mouse all at once! But Sabi had taken it in stride, returning her mother's hug before venturing out into the open. Now she was glad she had been given the reminders, though, staring up into the branches for a moment. No birds. Nodding in satisfaction she hurried on to her destination. Besides passing a few caterpillars and one extremely busy chipmunk who rushed up a tree nearby, Sabi found herself quite alone as she trundled to her destination. It was both freeing and terrifying to know.

Sooner than she cared to admit, she found herself approaching the dandelion patch. Soft cottony blooms wafted gently in the wind, some of the odd seeds breaking off and floating away to spread elsewhere. She had to pick them before they all blew away so Sabi hurriedly scooted herself up one of the stems. She settled into the billowy flower, relishing the feeling of sitting on a cloud for a moment. That was always the part of the story that had never frightened her: flying above the clouds. She was envious that birds got to enjoy such a spectacle on a daily basis.

Realizing she was daydreaming, Sabi quickly began picking the seeds and placing them in her basket. Checking the sky occasionally, the small mouse made sure to keep herself inconspicuous while gathering her bounty. Without anyone interrupting her or stealing her away to do other projects it took her almost no time at all to fill the basket, with plenty of seeds still left on the flower to come gather tomorrow. Extremely pleased with herself, Sabi glanced around once more before scuttling back to the earth.

Hurrying back to the shadows of a large oak tree, Sabi sat down and leaned against the trunk with a big sigh. She wasn't ready to go home yet, but she didn't want to be gone too long from the colony and worry her mother. Pricking her ears, she realized that she could hear a small trickle nearby. Figuring she had time to go and find the water source before she would be missed the young mouse gathered her basket and followed the gurgling sounds from the water. The grass became less dense as the noise grew louder and, before she knew it, she stepped out into full sunlight.

Blinking in surprise from the sudden brightness, Sabi let her eyes adjust before looking around her surroundings. It appeared to be a small creek, with rocks sticking up out of the swift-flowing water. Sniffing the air the young rodent could smell the moisture and mud in the air. Glancing both ways down the shore, she found paw prints of all types, including other mice, chipmunks, deer and what appeared to be an otter. However, she also noticed fox and weasel prints mixed in, making her fur stand up on the back of her neck. Better not spend too long here.

However, as she turned to go back, sunlight glinted off something resting on the bank. Curious, Sabi nearly dashed over to the object before remembering the rules. Crouching down she looked all around twice before venturing over to the object. Half-buried in the mud was something that sparkled as the sun's rays beat down on it. Gently prying it from the earth, she brought it over to the water to rinse off the excess muck still on it. Tiny minnows and tadpoles swam away in panic as her paws dipped beneath the surface into the cool liquid. Using a bit of moss to help scrub the object, once it was clean she lifted it out of the water to look at it better.

It appeared to be some sort of stone, both clear and green at once, with its multi-faceted surface fitting snugly in her paws. It was odd to see something that wasn't round or randomly shaped like the rocks she was used to. Whatever this stone was also heavier than a regular pebble of the same size. But the most bizarre thing was when the sun hit it, rainbows seemed to sprout in all directions, including on her fur. Gasping slightly, she placed the object in shadow and the rainbows disappeared, no matter how she turned it. Placing it in the sun again, the rainbows reappeared, bright and cheery in all directions.

Letting out a small squeak of amazement, she rushed back to where she had left her basket to put the odd stone in there. However, when she got back into the grasses she found that her basket had been knocked over. Suddenly on the alert, she held her breath and slowly twisted her ears about, trying to catch any sound. Scenting the wind she could tell someone else was nearby, though her untrained senses couldn't make out who or what it was. Anxiety started to creep into her body, which she tried to tamp down so she didn't panic.

"H-hello?" She asked quietly, hoping that whoever was out there was a friend.

Her hopes were quickly dashed as, not more than twenty paces away, the brown face of a weasel poked out of the grasses. A crude smile crossed his face as a long, lithe body came out into the open. Sharp fangs gleamed in the sunlight as small but powerful paws began creeping towards her. "Hello, little one." He stated calmly, though a predatory growl was low in his throat. "Do you happen to have any dinner plans?"

Too terrified to speak, Sabi backed away slowly, not wanting to attract more attention. However, the weasel guessed what she was trying to do and dove into the grasses, hiding himself in the vegetation. Whiskers trembling, Sabi retreated to the water's edge to enable her to see when the predator was coming. She could hear him rustling but in her panic it seemed to be coming from everywhere at once. Her paws became a death grip around the odd stone, as if that alone could save her. Maybe if she threw it that would distract the weasel, but she highly doubted such a master hunter would fall for such a simple tactic.

Suddenly, the rustling increased in volume and the weasel appeared again at a full dash. Letting out a high-pitched squeak, Sabi did the only thing she could think of: she dove into the water. Rushing to where the water ran deeper, she flung herself into it, her head disappearing under the surface within a moment. Kicking strongly, Sabi broke the surface and took a huge breath. Turning about frantically she didn't see the weasel anywhere…but she also had no idea where she was heading. Her head bobbed under the water again and she kicked towards the near bank in a feeble attempt to reach the shore again. Fish and frogs swam by, uncaring and unwilling (or unable) to help her.

Continuing with this method, taking huge gulps of air when she did surface, Sabi finally found her paws resting against a soft-feeling bottom. Using the last bit of her strength, she forced herself to wade out of the fast current. Gasping for breath, she collapsed on the now sandy bank. Amazingly, the odd stone was still in her hands, the water dripping off of it back into the creek. Glancing around, the small mouse felt her heart sink as she didn't recognize any of the landmarks nearby, even as she realized that the weasel was no longer around either. Even if she wasn't going to get eaten, now she was lost! She could always follow the water back to where she left her basket, but she had no idea how far away that was. If she didn't reach the area before nightfall, then she would be easy picking for an owl or a fox.

Setting the stone on the ground next to her, the small mouse huddled into a small ball and began to cry. If she hadn't been so eager to be on her own she could be back at the colony with her mother and the rest of her family, safe and sound. Wiping tears from her eyes, she tried to see the positives of her situation but right now, she couldn't think of any. Burying her head into her hands, she didn't notice the rainbows that appeared as the sun shone off the odd stone…or the shadow that passed over her. Sniffling, Sabi was trying to pull herself together when a melodious voice intruded on her sorrow.

"Excuse me, little one? Is that shiny stone yours?"

Gasping slightly and almost giving herself the hiccups, Sabi jumped and looked up. Standing above her was a giant black bird, head tilted to one side. Her dark brown eyes appeared almost black above her dull orange beak. Gray feet gripped the ground gently, the razor sharp talons digging small furrows in the sand. Sabi felt her heart stop for a moment, figuring she had escaped one hunter to meet her demise at the wings of another. All of the scary stories she'd even been told about birds came flying to the forefront of her mind, causing her to freeze in place.

"Ummm…Miss?" The crow asked again, her voice lilting and polite. "Are you alright?"

It slowly dawned on Sabi that the crow was not here to eat her. In fact, once she wiped her tears away and looked into the bird's eyes, she saw that there was no malice there. On the contrary, she actually seemed to be concerned about Sabi and her problems. Gulping slightly, the small rodent stood up and pointed up the river. "I was being hunted, so I jumped in the water. Then I got swept downstream and now I don't know how to get home."

The bird slumped slightly, her wings unfolding a bit. "Oh, sweetie, I'm sorry to hear that." She glanced over at the odd stone for a moment before returning her gaze to Sabi. "Do you know any distinguishing landmarks near your home?"

Sabi nodded briskly, her fear of birds all but forgotten by the crow's polite nature. "Yes, there's a five-topped oak and a three-topped elm nearby. Oh! And a fallen willow tree. Our colony isn't too far from the roots."

"Ahh, I see." The crow clacked her beak together, eying the stone again. "Tell you what. If you trade me the shiny stone then I can bring you home. I know where that is." She pointed a wing in the general direction that Sabi knew her home was. "Deal?"

"Deal." Sabi stated quickly, willing to give anything to get back home. "But umm..how do you plan to do that?"

In answer, the large bird nestled herself onto the ground and nodded her head towards her back. Sabi's eyes widened and she gasped slightly, her heart beating faster. Was this really happening? Could it be true? Moving forward slowly, the crow unfurled a wing, allowing the small mouse a ramp to get to her back. Delighted, Sabi gently but firmly climbed onto the bird's back and grabbed a pawful of feathers. Standing back up again, the crow carefully walked over to the stone and gently grabbed it in her talons before turning to Sabi. "Are you all set? Got a good hold?"

Sabi nodded and suddenly the crow was flapping her wings hard, getting them airborne within seconds. The young rodent let out a squeak of excitement as they rose above the grasses, above the stones, even above the trees. Peering around at the vast expanse of empty air around her, she nearly whooped with delight at the wind blowing in her face and the wisps of cloud floating around her. Even the setting sun seemed so much larger and brighter up here. It was everything she had hoped for and all that she had imagined. However, one glance towards the earth made her realize that she should look to the side and not down. That was still terrifying!

All too soon, she saw the trees that she had mentioned, along with the small clearing that the crow was heading towards. Her colony was only a skip away from there and, as they gently drifted towards the ground, she could even see some of the colonists scurrying about. Bravely, she waved down at them, but the large bird had caused everyone to run into hiding... except one. Her mother, her face contorted in worry, stared in shocked fascination as the crow and mouse landed. As soon as Sabi scampered back down the outstretched wing she found herself in her mother's embrace.

"SABI!" She cried, nearly squeezing her ribs to pieces. "Where have you been?! I've been so worried!" Before Sabi could reply, however, her mother turned and bowed to the large crow. "Thank you for bringing my daughter home…"

"Sidian." The crow replied, clacking her beak in appreciation.

"Sidian. Thank you for bringing her back." Her mother boldly reached out and pat the large birds talons.

"I can't turn away a young one crying, now, can I?" Sidian answered. Then she held up the odd stone. "Plus she pays well. Be careful out there." She flapped her wings to get airborne again, circling around once she found a decent air current. "But if you ever find anything else shiny, don't hesitate to call."

As Sidian flew away, Sabi felt herself crushed in her mother's embrace. "Sabi, Sabi. Where have you been?"

"Oh Mother." Sabi stated, fiercely hugging her back before they began heading into the nest. "Have I got a story to tell you."

Gharial: A Riddle Poem
by Marlowe Whittenberg

I have nobs on my narrow snout
I have over one hundred teeth

I am the world's largest reptile
I am the closest living relative to the dinosaurs

I like to eat fish, small mammals, and frogs
I like to swim, crawl, and run

I live in deep rivers and sand banks in India
I live my life through the night, sleeping during the day

I can mate under water
I can puff out my neck

I am hunted for my skin and meat
I am turned into shoes, wallets, and souvenirs

There's only 200 left of me in the wild...

(I wish there were more)
(I miss my friends and family)

Who am I?

Notes: I picked the gharial because I like the saw shark and reptiles and the gharial is a combination of them both. Plus, the gharial is huge. It can get up to 20 feet long and weigh up to 1,500 pounds.

Over two billion dollars' worth of crocodile products are sold each year. I'm sad and mad because people are killing these gharials and other reptiles.

Scientists are working with gharials in captivity to help them mate so there will be more of them.

I would like to join the Convention of International Trade on Endangered Species (CITES) and the International Union for the Conservation of Nature (INCN) to help protect them.

Thank you to the helpful, knowledgeable staff at the Academy of Natural Science of Drexel University for the information I gathered on crocodiles, endangered animals and our endangered planet.

Day 5 - Chipmunks
by Esther Fishman

We wake thinking about leaving. These trips
are always too short. Today we have to
pack up. Somehow, all the equipment that
makes it possible to survive up here—tents,
sleeping bags, propane burners, assorted
rope and tarps and boots—have to fit back
into the tiny, rented car so that
we can drive home. As always, we have too
much food, and it's not worth taking home,
so David dumps little piles

discreetly around the outskirts of our
camp. Even the dog leaves them alone, full
of last night's leftovers. "Well, someone will
eat it." He empties out the pot of old
mac and cheese. It sits on the big rock,
looking utterly alien in its
lurid orangeness. "Nothing's going to eat
that," comments the mother-in-law. It sits.
We continue cleaning up the camp. An
atmosphere of melancholy sets in.

Suddenly I see the little chipmunks
that inhabit the area running
around on the rock. Maybe they will
become interested in the mac and
cheese. One is drinking water from the pot,
holding on to the rim with prehensile
back paws. Another one grabs a piece of
macaroni with what can only be
described as hands and nibbles it
tentatively. Then, it seems everyone

wants some, because soon there are six or
seven of them, running up to the pile
of mac and cheese, grabbing a piece, and
running off with it stuffed in their cheeks. Quite

a show, and soon we are all watching,
trying not to scare them away by
laughing too loud or moving suddenly.
"How much can those tiny stomachs hold at
one time?" I wonder out loud. "Maybe they

are squirreling it away," says the
poet husband, who is responsible
for the feast being available in
the first place. That little bit of wordplay
is all that is necessary—-we
begin free-associating a
mythology for these cute little
creatures as they run around, chewing
furiously. Now that they are in
possession of the orange creamy goodness

that is our discarded mac and cheese, we
imagine a new life for them in the
coming winter, a new group of super-
chipmunks who will worship the orange stuff that
came from above. Isn't that just like us
humans, making story out of just stuff
that happens. We anthropomorphize at
the drop of a hat, spinning
complexity as if it were the stuff
of nature. It's easy because we will

not be here to find out what really
happens. We can cast ourselves as
beneficent gods, bestowing some kind
of boon when we really have no idea
what goes on underground in rodent dens
when the snow lies thick over this ground and
the wind blows down the mountain. For all we
know, we have killed them all, poisoned them with
food that we, after all, rejected.

Early Evening
by Lynette G. Esposito

Sun contemplates the language
of landscape at twilight
as a thread of light
encircles the horizon.

The calm orb slides down its
nightly path
pulls the silken imaginary curtain
over imaginary time
while fox babies feast
beside their sleeping mother.

94 *Horse Sculpture - Roger Camp*

BIOS

AJD
AJD is currently without work and is, usually, obnoxiously content -- quite grateful for many undeserved mercies. Not all lights in the tunnel are worth pursuing. Talk first at 1-800-273-8255.

MICHAEL BALDWIN
Michael Baldwin, is a native of Fort Worth, TX. A retired library administrator and professor of American Government, his poetry was featured on the national radio program *The Romantic Hours*, and has twice been nominated for the Pushcart Prize. He won the Violet Newton Single Poem Prize, 2000, the Eakin Award, 2011 for *Scapes*, and the Morris Chapbook Award, 2012, for *Counting Backward From Infinity*. His book of Texas poetry, *Lone Star Heart* (Lamar University Press, 2016), vied for the Texas Institute of Letters Poetry Book Award. His third poetry book, *The Quantum Uncertainty of Love* (Shanti Arts Press, 2019) received a Readers Favorite 5-Star Award. Mr. Baldwin resides in Benbrook, TX.

SARAH BARTLETT
Sarah Bartlett lives in Seattle, WA. Her recent chapbook, *Columbarium*, was released in 2019 by dancing girl press. Her poetry collection, *Sometimes We Walk With Our Nails Is Out*, was released in 2016 by Subito Press. She is the author of two chapbooks, *My Only Living Relative*, published by Phantom Books in 2015, and *Freud Blah Blah Blah*, published by Rye House Press in 2014. She is also co-author of two collaborative chapbooks. Recent work has appeared in *Eratio*, *PEN American Poetry Series*, *Poetry Daily*, *Lit*, *Boog City*, *Alice Blue*, and elsewhere.

ARNOLD B. CABDRIVER
Long Beach (Washington, not California) native, Cabdriver takes inspiration from the wildlife around him, the wildlife far below him when he's out in his boat, and the wildlife he used to see as a child during his short visits to the Oregon Zoo. Cabdriver has been a writer-in-residence at the Sou'wester on fifteen separate occasions. And still nobody remembers him!

Roger Camp

Roger Camp is the author of three photography books including the award-winning *Butterflies in Flight* (Thames & Hudson, 2002) and *Heat* (Charta, Milano, 2008). His work has appeared in numerous journals including *The New England Review*, *New York Quarterly*, and the *Vassar Review*. He previously worked as a reference librarian at the Santa Ana Public Library and as an analytical bibliographer for the director of the Humanities Research Center at the University of Texas, Austin.

Yuan Changming

Yuan Changming edits *Poetry Pacific* with Allen Yuan in Vancouver. Credits include Pushcart nominations, poetry awards as well as publications in *Best of the Best Canadian Poetry* (2008-17), & *BestNewPoemsOnline*, among others.

Mickey Collins

~~Mickey rights wrongs. Mickey wrongs rites.~~ Mickey writes words, sometimes wrong words but he tries to get it write.

Desiree Ducharme

Desiree Ducharme is a writer. Her semi-voluntary, health-adjacent sabbatical has ended. She has returned to full time employment at Powell's City of Books in a dragon-adjacent capacity. She resumed her previous schedule of imagining nonsense while on public transportation, which is less populated yet somehow more post-apocalypse-y than it was in March. She spends her days verbally and non-verbally asking people to fix their masks and step back. She longs for a day where she can complain about her "buyer's wing" being sore. So, fix your mask and step back. Read more words at her website desireeducharme.com

Lynette G. Esposito

Lynette G. Esposito has been an Adjunct Professor at Rowan University, Burlington County and Camden County Colleges. She has taught creative writing and conducted workshops in New Jersey and Pennsylvania. Mrs. Esposito holds a BA in English from the University of Illinois and an MA in Creative Writing and English Literature from Rutgers University. Her articles have appeared in the national publication, *Teaching for Success*; regionally in *South Jersey Magazine*, *SJ Magazine*, *Delaware Valley Magazine*, and her essays have appeared in *Reader's Digest* and *The Philadelphia Inquirer*. Her poetry has appeared in *US1*, *SRN Review*, *The Foxchase Review*, *Remembered Arts*, *Poetry Quarterly* and other literary magazines and journals. She has critiqued poetry for local and regional writer's conferences and served as a panelist and speaker at local and national writer's conferences. She lived with her husband, Attilio, in Mount Laurel, NJ.

ROBERT EVERSMANN
Robert Eversmann works for Deep Overstock. His website is roberteversmann.com

ESTHER FISHMAN
I have published reviews on the web at thereviewreview.net and raintaxi.com. My poetry has appeared in various small magazines, most recently *Bloodroot Literary Magazine.*

HEATHER GLOVER
My name is Heather Glover and I am a 32 year old woman living with MS. I am currently querying a full-length YA fantasy manuscript and was published several years ago in the *All-American Writers* journal. I was also part of the query-matching team for Camp RevPit during spring 2020.

MICHAL GOLDSTEIN
As a recent high school graduate and student in Harvard University's class of 2025, I've committed myself to working on my writing throughout my gap year. My poem on gender, "blank canvases," has been featured as an Editor's Choice Award in *Teen Ink*'s magazine, and I have worked with my school's library to host a celebration of student authors annually. I am most proud of works of literary research, notably my paper about Holocaust art, titled "How We Silence Voices of the Holocaust: Jewish Women in Art and Female Representation in Holocaust Memorials."

JOHN GREY
John Grey is an Australian poet, US resident, recently published in *Soundings East, Dalhousie Review* and *Connecticut River Review.* Work upcoming in *Hollins Critic, Redactions* and *I-70 Review.*

ARIEL KUSBY
Ariel Kusby is a writer and bookseller based in Portland, OR. Her poems, stories, and reviews have appeared in *Entropy, The Adroit Journal, Queen Mob's Teahouse, Bone Bouquet, SUSAN / The Journal, Bodega Magazine, Hunger Mountain,* and *Pom Pom Lit Mag,* amongst others, and she has been nominated for a Pushcart Prize. She is the author of the children's book *The Little Witch's Book of Spells* (Chronicle, 2020), and the founder of Little Witchery, a magical community for children and adults. Visit her website at www.arielkusby.com.

Kellye McBride
Kellye McBride is a freelance writer, editor, and film instructor from the Portland area. She currently serves as the TV editor for the UK horror blog *Sublime Horror* and has written for numerous film publications, including *Rue Morgue* magazine, *Scream* magazine, and *Horror Homeroom*. She's been previously published in *Stephen King and Philosophy*. Her short nonfiction has been recently nominated for the Bram Stoker Awards by the Horror Writer's Association.

Azalea Micketti
Azalea is a writer, director, actor, and bookseller living in the weirdest place on earth (open for heated discussion). She loves words, knows a little too much about Shakespeare, and will happily discuss books for literal hours.

Walter Moon
walter moon has been lost in books since birth and bookselling in one way or another for almost 20 years. living in portland with his partner, Nat, and their companion, Mishka, he strives to find the key to immortality but has trouble locating the key to his house.

Fabrice Poussin
Fabrice Poussin teaches French and English at Shorter University. Author of novels and poetry, his work has appeared in *Kestrel*, *Symposium*, *The Chimes*, and many other magazines. His photography has been published in *The Front Porch Review*, the *San Pedro River Review* as well as other publications.

Kezia Rasmussen
Zuriel and Kezia are sisters, who share a home, job, some pets, and many whimsical hobbies... along with Zuriel's husband. It is an unconventional lifestyle that surely has neighbors confused. We like it that way.

Michael Santiago
Michael Santiago is a serial expat, avid traveler, and writer of all kinds. Originally from New York City, and later relocating to Rome in 2016 and Nanjing in 2018. He enjoys the finer things in life like walks on the beach, existential conversations and swapping murder mystery ideas. Keen on exploring themes of humanity within a fictitious context and aspiring author.

Bob Selcrosse
Bob Selcrosse grew up with his mother, selling books, in the Pacific Northwest. He is now working on a book about a book. It is based in the Pacific Northwest. The book is *The Cabinet of Children*.

Jihye Shin
Jihye Shin is a 1.5-generation Korean-American bookseller in Florida. Her work focuses on the poetics of the analog-digital, liminial and futurist differences. She is also the creator of a text-based interactive game called Goodnight, Starlight. Her professional website is www.jihyeshin.ink.

G Michael Smith
G Michael Smith is a poet, a novelist and children's book author. He has a BA in Psychology, English and Creative Writing and a professional teaching degree from the University of British Columbia. He has a Masters of Arts degree from San Diego State University.
He has written four science fiction novels in The Forevers series all featuring a young female protagonist; mid-grade novel titled "Hijacked - A Beechwood Adventure"; written and illustrated three children's books titled "The Accidental Adventures of Bernie the Banana Slug", "Lily Liar and the Eleventy Headed Monster" and "Tiny Tina and the Terrible Trouble". Website - https://gmsmithbooks.ca.

Eric Thralby
Captain by trade, Cpt. Eric Thralby works wood in his long off-days. He time-to-time pilots the Bremerton Ferry (Bremerton—Vashon; Vahon—Bremerton), while other times sells books on amazon.com, SellerID: plainpages. He'll sell any books the people love, strolling down to library and yard sales, but he loves especially books of Romantic fiction, not of risqué gargoyles, not harlequin romance, but knights, errant or of the Table. Eric has not published before, but has read in local readings at the Gig Harbor Candy Company and the Lavender Inne, also in Gig Harbor.

Robert Torres
Robert Torres is a writer and performer based in Portland, Oregon who has worked with Monkey with a Hat On, Fuse Theatre Ensemble, and Twilight Theater Company, and has been published by *Entropy*, *Nailed Magazine*, *1001 Journal*, *Spider Web Salon*, and others. They worked for three years as a bookseller at Black Hat Books in Portland. Their work explores anxiety, delusion, revolution, and the conundrum of having a body whether you like it or not.

Jonathan van Belle
Jonathan van Belle is a copy editor for Outlier.org, an online education platform. He previously worked as a bookseller at Powell's City of Books. Jonathan is the author of several books, all available online, and is currently working on his first book for Deep Overstock Publishing.

Zuriel van Belle
Zuriel van Belle mostly thinks about people, places, and animals. She is currently focused on improving canine-feline relations in Milwaukie, Oregon.

Z.B. Wagman
Z.B. Wagman is a writer based in Portland, Oregon. He has two dogs that take most of his attention. When not bribing the dogs out into the rain, he can be found at the Beaverton City Library, where he finds much inspiration for his writing.

George White
George White is a Creative Writing graduate from the north of England. She enjoys writing flash fiction but she also dabbles in ekphrastic and dystopian fiction. She splits her time between writing creatively and writing blog posts about what has caught her eye in the media.

Marlowe Whittenberg
Marlowe Whittenberg is an avid soccer player. He loves graphic novels and hopes to be a botanist someday.

Nicholas Yandell
Nicholas Yandell is a composer, who sometimes creates with words instead of sound. In those cases, he usually ends up with fiction and occasionally poetry. He also paints and draws, and often all these activities become combined, because they're really not all that different from each other, and it's all just art right?
When not working on creative projects, Nick works as a bookseller at Powell's Books in Portland, Oregon, where he enjoys being surrounded by a wealth of knowledge, as well as working and interacting with creatively stimulating people. He has a website where he displays his creations; it's nicholasyandell.com. Check it out!

All rights to the works contained in this journal belong to their respective authors. Any ideas or beliefs presented by these authors do not necessarily reflect the ideas or beliefs held by Deep Overstock's *editors.*

CPSIA information can be obtained
at www.ICGtesting.com
Printed in the USA
FSHW010904030121
77356FS